**BOOK SIX OF THE
RIM CONFEDERACY**

Desert Planet

by Jim Rudnick

RUDNICK PRESS

Desert Planet

Cover art by Sebastian Wagner.

ISBN-13: 978-1-988144-06-1
Copyright © 2016
Jim Rudnick

RUDNICK PRESS

For my Susan...

Desert Planet

The RIM Confederacy: Desert Planet

"After 55 years of waiting for an answer to the invite to join the RIM Confederacy, the planet Enki has responded with an alternate idea—that the RIM Confederacy join them instead. Captain Tanner Scott is sent on the Diplomatic mission to get the Enkians to reconsider.

What he and the Atlas crew do is to help the new Ambassador to find a way to both diplomatic as well as the Enki into the RIM Confederacy without exposing to them the secret of why that is so important. If the Enkians can be persuaded, the RIM could gain access to the newly discovered metal ores that appear to make a ship invulnerable.

But all of the RIM wants to shortcut the process so the Atlas needs to quarantine the planet as well as maintain full diplomacy with the Enkians. When the Caliphate gets involved and back room deals are made it all comes to a head at the Atlas Adept Officers trial for Terrorism.

Captain Scott will try to defend his officer by acting as his defense counsel—a job that is made even more difficult as the Enkian society and justice system are both hard to learn and hard to navigate within the law..."

Desert Planet

A Message to you from the Author...

I just wanted to say thanks so so much for reading Book Six of the RIM Confederacy!

As my Amazon bio says, being a youngster in the 1950's meant that I was a voracious reader in what has been called the Golden Age of Science Fiction. That meant that for me, my heroes were not on the hockey rink or gridiron - but instead in my local Library where at 12 I had a full Adult card (thanks Dad!) and took out more than 5 books a week.

Everyone from Heinlein, Norton, Leiber, Pohl, Anderson, Simak, Asimov, Brackett, Gunn, Van Vogt and more....I fell in love with and eventually owned Ace Doubles of my own.

And while I never knew who wrote the Tom Corbett - Space Cadet series, I fell in love with them and they had a place of honor on my own bookcase too!

With that kind of an introduction to Science Fiction, it's no wonder that when I got my writing work done, I turned my own fictional side of my brain to writing same. It's one thing I know how to write - and a totally different matter to release same to the world - something that I've just started to work on....

Suffice it to say my own works are rooted in that Golden Age and it's that era that I'd like to one day be known as a teensy contributor to in some small way...

So once again, thanks for beginning my RIM Confederacy series and wait'll you learn about the alcoholic spaceship captain that is my hero, who fights and beats aliens but not the bottle!

Enjoy and remember, in a series, characters develop and mature not the way we sometimes want...instead, it's like they have a life of their own!

And a gentle reminder — this is not alien

invasions and space battles — instead it truly is tales from the RIM about the people who inhabit and live and love and win and lose on the RIM!

And while you can read the series in any order, I'd highly recommend to start with Pirates, then Sleeper Ship, Prison Planet, Ancient Relics, Hospital Ship and Desert Planet too...and yes, there's more coming soon too!

Desert Planet

Prologue ~

The lines on the access ramps had been long, yet thousands had stood at first in the sands, then later on the stone walkway, and finally had used the steps to go down, down into the depths of the planet and still they came. Following each other, they finally reached the lowest levels, and as the huge wide corridor slowly doubled back on itself toward the Words Muse pyramid, they slowed with the sheer numbers of observers who had come. It was hot, as it always was, and some fanned themselves with flyers, which had been distributed about this Claim, trying to cool off even a bit but to no avail. At least they were all out of the hot white sun, an A1, which meant it was almost at the top of the white class of stars with hot, hot stellar winds that landed on Enki.

Being third in orbit around the sun was just poor luck, many thought, as that made the sun even brighter and hotter. Enki lay at the interior edge of the Goldilocks zone, which meant the sun always shone and the heat was always there. Here in the darkened tunnel that ran from the exterior access ramp to the Words pyramid, it was usually at least somewhat cooler, but now with thousands of Enkians all surging forward to get to the Claims forum, it was just plain hot.

Eventually the long lines reached the basement level of the pyramid and slowly climbed the stairs back up to the main ground floor level. As a unit, they all followed one another and took seats in the huge Claims forum that made up most of the ground level of the pyramid. There was seating for thousands and every single seat was filled, and there was standing room too, but it was filled — jammed really. Everyone who was close enough to the area in general, never mind the pyramid itself, was here. Major news services were present too, broadcasting the jurors and their decision on the Claims action filed by the Words Muse.

All eyes were turned on the three groups seated at the triangular table on the dais in the middle of the forum. One side held the jurors — the five members of the ruling judicial power on Enki. One side held the Words Muse leaders, four men and a woman who held those positions. The third and final side of the table held the five leaders of the Performance Muse, the ones who had brought the action of the Claim.

All this was because a message had been received from the RIM Confederacy inviting them to join.

The Performance Muse had claimed it was they who had been asked, as the message had come via a video recording, which showed an ambassador who read the parchment, but it was the video that was the deciding factor. Or so they said in their argument just a few weeks ago.

The Words Muse claimed that as the message also had come as a beautiful letter on parchment paper with embossed seals and all, it was a word message that had invited them. It had been read, but as the message was in words—it was meant for them, they had argued.

And today, the jurors would pronounce their decision.

The head juror, Iavoesi Qax, his crest of feathers along the top of his head bright green with the yellow borders, was old but still carried himself like a mature Enkian. He rippled his crest from flat back up to standing tall again and again, and that got the quiet he'd been looking for.

"Enkians, the jurors have been considering this Claim by the Performance and Words, and we have come to a decision, one that was difficult, but one that we are sure takes into consideration the full bearing of this RIM Confederacy message," he said as he looked at both sides in front of him.

On the Words side, the red and white feathered crests were full and preened up; it was obvious the Words Muse felt they had won the Claim to the message. On the Performance side of the table, the crests were not as high; instead, the purple and orange crests were a bit droopy, their beaks were gritted together, and not one was smiling.

The head juror looked down at his Agenda, and then rising, he stood fully—and then leaned over to the Words side of the table and threw back his head to caw loudly the jurors' verdict three times. "Words, Words, Words."

Nods were seen all around the forum. Everyone thought this was the proper decision. Everyone now knew the WORDS muse was meant to be the recipient of the RIM Confederacy message. The Words Muse would handle the talks and discussions, and as they had been the recipients, this RIM Confederacy would be able to join the Words Muse.

The head of the Words muse then stood to relate to all present that they would be contacting this RIM Confederacy to discuss how they could join their muse and informing the jurors soonest. The Claim forum was over and all present took their leave back down to the tunnels and then out to the sands.

In Resources, the probe was made ready, and it blasted off with the Words' message the only thing inside as it climbed up and out of the atmosphere as it found its bearings and aimed itself at Juno.

It took a year to reach its top speed of one-half the speed of light ... and in fifty-five years, it would reach Juno to respond to the RIM message.

Desert Planet

CHAPTER ONE

Over Juno in high orbit, Station One was in a sorry state; budgets had just been tendered to the admiral down in Navy Hall, and all had come back with a single word—cut!

Marine Master Sergeant Bill Adams, the officer of the day on the bridge, didn't much care. As his job was not dependent on the pluses or minuses of the operations of the station, all he had to do was get through an eight-hour shift. Every day, the same eight hours and then to the non-commissioned Officers' Mess for a few brewskis and to sleep it off before doing it all over again and again.

Life's good, he thought, as he checked his command console again and noted the all-green status of every single icon on the screen. *Air's fine;*

power's fine; communication's fine; and orbit is fine—all is fine. And beer is only an hour away. The whole furor about budgets and the now necessary cuts that were on everyone's lips meant nothing to him. This was a simple six-month duty for him—part of the tour from specialist training, so budgets be damned.

Talk about "lucking-in," he thought. His final year in upper school, a teacher had taken him off to one side and had prompted him—pushed him in fact— to apply to the Officers Candidate School over on Eons. They tried to turn him into a Navy officer— and while it had made sense for some time, in the end, he couldn't do it.

Instead, he'd forgone the option of the life of an officer and had enlisted on his graduation day at a Navy recruiting office in his home city of Hamilton down on Juno. "Joined up," he said to himself, "and breezed through basic, took weapons specialty training, made marksman, and now here on Station One, crew chief at thirty-one." He smiled, sipped a gulp of his bottled water, and then slid the re-sealed bottle back into the cup holder on his chair.

'Tisn't a captain's chair, that's true, but then that went with officer territory. Instead, I will one day lead a squad out in the field, and that's where I belong, he thought. *'Til then, it's a green-screen shift followed by some beers.* He shrugged and looked over at some of the crew on this shift with him.

In charge of the Station Control—well, at least as far as having control of thrusters and the ilk as there were no engines on the station—was sergeant Mel Backert, who like Bill, had also enlisted and had pulled six-month duty on the station too. "Good man," Bill said to himself and noted Mel's attention appeared to be down on his own console at his station.

Glancing up at the huge view-screen on the forward wall, he saw what he always saw—the curved edge of Juno with its blue oceans and white puffy cloud bans off to port. Ahead, as they were on the outer side of the planet, they could see most of the inward-facing stars of the RIM Confederacy and, much smaller, the wide band of muddied stars that was the rest of the galaxy. From this far out, more than fifty thousand lights, the galaxy was just an unfocused band of shining stars that numbered in the billions. "We're just a pimple on the butt of the Milky Way," he said to himself as he swigged from his bottled water and half-turned to his right to see what others were doing on the bridge. *Keeps Mel busy, I'd guess.*

His Science officer, Corporal Harry Neal was busy reading something like all Science officers were always doing, and his concentration looked intense. His Ansible officer, one Phil Sibbald, was using his throat mic, most likely to talk to someone.

Wonder if that rank promotion would come through, he thought, as he'd also added his own recommendations to Phil's file months ago—should happen soon, he hoped. *Another good man.*

Beep, beep, beep. An alarm went off and the sidebar on the huge view-screen held a flashing icon that meant trouble.

"Sir, collision alarm—we've got incoming something," his Science officer jumped in first.

"Sir," the Ansible officer said, "no response to hails—in fact, they don't even have an Ansible device address, Sir," Phil said with wonder in his voice.

"Sir," his Station Control officer said, "it's ...wait, yes, it is braking big time ... slowing ... and it's now not on a collision course, Sir," Mel said with relief in his voice.

Bill thought the braking was odd—no natural item could brake it's vector—and without an Ansible address, it had to be a natural item, an asteroid or meteor or some such rock.

He looked over at his Science crewman and nodded to him first. "Get me a read on what that is STAT."

To his Ansible officer he was just as curt. "Ansible down to Juno—major security interrupt code Station-RR-Alpha—and blast that 'til you get an acknowledgment and tactical orders. STAT,

19

Phil, STAT!"

Back to his station control man, Mel, he said,
"Can we locate it and put it up on screen? Front and
center and put up some kind of a measurement too
on this thing, and get me vitals too."

All eyes were now on that view-screen as it went
black as the cameras changed, and on screen, a
silver missile appeared, coming in tail first as it
slowed even more, according to the sidebar stats. It
was a rocket, a missile, or a probe, and it was
approximately forty feet long with a radius of about
nine feet. Vitals popped on screen too as the station
scanned the intruder, and Bill saw the stats showed
no life onboard, no air or life signs, and no cargo
except an almost empty reservoir of what must be
fuel.

His Science officer chimed in. "Sir, that thing is
not a RIM Confederacy ... uh, probe at all. Scans
show that it is made of a metal that we do not know
—never seen that chem spectroscopy before. Also
while there is a single compartment up front, it
appears to have nothing in it but some organics, but
without a trip over there, we've no idea," he said
and Bill could hear the plea to be a part of that team
from Harry.

He held up his hand. "Ansible and Tactical—did
you get any feedback from Navy Hall?" he said.

Both officers shook their heads.

"Tactical—Bertie, can you lock on that ... uh, probe—let's call it a probe. Can you lock on with station energy pulse cannon on the starboard side and put that up on screen too?" he said.

As she nodded back to him and said, "Wilco," the sidebar up on the screen added the station energy pulse readouts. On screen, a set of cross hairs ringed the probe and a small pulse volume bar appeared.

"All the way," Bill said, and he too watched as the bar doubled in size indicating maximum charges would be applied.

"And now we wait," he said and that's what they did.

The sidebar indicators never changed.

The probe didn't move but joined the station in its slow high orbit around Juno as physics said it should.

The crew waved off their shift replacements and all agreed to stay with this.

After more than three hours of the standoff, there was a beep on the command console and the admiral's face appeared.

It was an EYES ONLY for him alone.

"Master Sergeant, Adams—Admiral McQueen here. What's the status currently? Anything new?" he said.

A man of late middle age, the admiral was the

head of the RIM Confederacy Navy—the commander in chief—so this was a first for Bill.

"Sir, yes ... no changes to the status of the probe, Sir. We are watching and monitoring carefully and yes, sending down the data to Navy control. We have seen not a single change since the probe braked about three hours ago, Sir," Bill said.

The admiral nodded and Bill thought he looked like any commander in chief. *Gray hair, slightly longer than Navy code allowed, but then who was going to tell him?* That almost brought a smile to his face, but he stifled that immediately.

McQueen half-turned and said something to someone else wherever he was and then turned back to the screen.

"Master Sergeant, I'm sending orders now—but here's the gist of this. I want you to form an away team, get over to this ... this probe, and take it aboard. I want it kept securely on Station One, and I want a full double platoon of marines—I'm sending them up now—on guard. No one to go near this probe until my own scientists and security arrives. You got that, Master Sergeant?"

There is no doubt the admiral is trying to fix in his own mind that I'm capable of doing just this. No more. No less.

"Sir, yes, Sir! Will follow those orders to the letter. Yes Sir!" he said and if he could have come to attention, he would have.

The screen went dark and Bill sat for a moment.

"Science, front and center, please," he said.

From behind him, Harry Neal jumped out of his seat and took up station off to his right. His hair was white, as all Conclusion citizens had white hair, and Bill noted he at least kept the long white hair on the back of each of his hands cut very short. He loved Science, which Bill knew, and hence his decision was easy.

"Corporal, you will assemble an away team to take out our large cargo shuttle to close with that probe, take it on board, bring it back to the station, and then place it in max security—full force five force-fields all around it in landing port four. You are to do nothing to the probe-no investigations, no entry—nothing—do you read me, Corporal?" he said, his voice hard and edged.

Harry knew this was both important and perhaps a matter of life and death. He snapped to attention and saluted. "Aye, Sir—Wilco and I will ensure that there is no byplay between us and the probe, Sir," he said and Bill could tell he meant that.

About ten minutes went by and then appearing on the screen in front of the bridge crew, the cargo shuttle moved into view as it swung over the top of the probe and came to a direct halt. While the bridge crew couldn't see it, the cargo doors along the side of the shuttle must have opened as the probe suddenly turned neon magenta as the tractor beam played out on it. Slowly the probe lifted toward the cargo shuttle and disappeared inside.

Careful eyes followed that move on the view-screen sidebar, and not a single thing changed. The probe was appeared to still be asleep.

As the cargo shuttle slowly yawed toward the station cameras, it gently and cautiously moved toward the station.

It disappeared after a minute or so and Bill said, "Landing port four, please, Station Control."

Mel punched some monitor buttons, and the landing bay came into view. Large enough to hold a dozen of those cargo shuttles that ran more than one hundred feet in length, it had just been cleared, and the only other vehicle there was a marine shuttle that had just arrived up from Juno. Awaiting the arrival of the station cargo shuttle were more than four dozen marines, in full gear and armor, and all armed with everything from Merkels to Ship-Busters. *Armed and aware should be their motto,* Bill thought as the cargo shuttle slowly entered the landing port.

Whomever Harry had chosen for the pilot, this guy was good. He swung the shuttle so slowly that it looked like it was in slow motion. But eventually it had swung in between the force-field stanchions that had been placed and positioned carefully. As the shuttle came to rest, the whole side panel slid up, and from the ceiling of the landing port, that magenta ray came out to slowly lift the probe out of the cargo shuttle hold and move it onto the deck of the bay. It again happened slowly and Bill's eyes went back and forth from the live feed on the view-screen to the sideboard vitals, and there was no change at all. The probe was truly asleep, he figured, and that was surely a good thing.

As the magenta ray of the tractor beam snapped out, the blue force-field shimmers went up around the probe, and everyone let out a breath.

"Sir," came a message from the shuttle, "permission to disembark here and join the team up from Juno, Sir."

While Bill didn't hear a please with that message, he surely knew there was an implied one. "Granted, Corporal Neal. Send the rest of the team on their way, and I want your full report on my console within the hour, 10-4, Corporal?" he said and received a "Wilco" back.

Taking a moment, he went back to his console, entered his search term at Gallipedia, and turned back to the crew.

"Ansible, all feeds sent and received down to Navy Hall, yes?" he said and Phil nodded back and said, "Roger, Sir."

"Station Control, set view back to normal and archive those feeds since the alarms. Make a double copy and stream that down to Juno too," he said.

"Tactical, as you're closest, get us another Science officer up here—I take it that we're going to be here for at least another few hours—so first round down in Non-com Mess is on me then. 'Til then, I want reports from everyone on my console within an hour. Anything—and I mean anything that you noticed or found or saw or figured out on your own —I want that in your report. No exceptions— anything and everything here, folks," he said as he looked down at his search results on his console monitor.

He looked around at everyone. "So far, there has never been such an event before, Gallipedia reports. No such an event ever—on the RIM, that is. We were not attacked, but we still had an incoming intruder get by all our RIM border defenses. All of them. This is important, folks. So if you've anything to report—do that. Nothing is dumbass or stupid either. I want what you experienced and I want it unadulterated and raw. Capisce?" he said and his voice was as persuasive as he could make it.

All the crew turned back to their stations and heads dropped as they began to work on those reports.

And then I gotta write my own too, Bill thought, *and*

all I saw was nothing other than what the recordings would show ...

#####

It had taken almost three weeks to get the task force together. Half an hour ago, the three ships under the flag of the RIM Navy and were finally on their way and leaving Juno. With the ability to go triple the speed of either the *DN Triumph,* a frigate, or the *RN Marwick,* a cruiser, the *Atlas* had agreed the task force speed was one light a day. The trip would take approximately twenty-seven days to get to Enki.

Sitting in the captain's chair once more, Tanner grinned to himself. Even the slow speed would be a great way to spend a *month or so; anything is better than twiddling my thumbs on the Barony Hospital Ship, anything!* There had been changes in his life—that was a given.

One of which—he smiled wryly—*was the list of items to think on from my psychiatrist. Things to try to understand about those ninety days I spent on the Hospital Ship while doctors tested me to make sure I was sane.*

Sane he was. Poorer but sane.

The court proceedings—the final voice on whether or not he was sane, as if there was any doubt—had found him sane. All the doctors agreed.

The charges against him of the assault of all those marines was mitigated somewhat and fines were levied. Large fines, which just about emptied his account for rainy-day money. But then the Baroness had given him a surprise one-time payment of a full year's captain's pay for his work on the Ghayth project. The fact that he'd found what was proving to be working anti-gravity devices should have been worth more, he sniffed to himself, but a year's pay was a year's pay.

He took another sip of the green tea in his plas-cup and grimaced. The psychiatrist had told him it might help if he tried to break some habits. His love of the double-double coffees on the bridge was just one of those items, hence the move to green tea. Yesterday he'd had three different Earl Grey varieties and had hated them all. The day before, it had been Darjeeling, and he hadn't even been able to finish one cup.

Tea sucks, he thought, and *I'm not going to find a kind I like—at least so far. So, if I can't find something that I like in say five minutes ... nah*—he shook his head—*say during this whole trip to Enki, then I'm back to my double-doubles. End of story.* He nodded to himself and looked over at his helmsman, Lieutenant Cooper.

"Helm, please make a note for me in my captain's log? Remind me that if I do not find a substitute for my double-doubles by the time we get to Enki, then tea will be banned on the *Atlas*. Make that a big bloody reminder," he said as he forced down another swallow of the green tea.

"Aye, Sir—noted and logged and it'll come up on the captain's console soon as we hit orbit around Enki. Might I add, Sir, that I never liked that stuff either," Randy Cooper said and grinned back at his captain.

Randy had been his main helmsman since his very first shift on the bridge of the *Atlas*, and Tanner liked his take on controlling the ship. Tanner looked around the bridge and smiled.

All of his crew was still on the *Atlas,* and all held their allegiance to him as a personal goal. He looked over at the Ansible station and smiled at the back of Lieutenant Irving's head—she had been instrumental in helping thwart the Caliphate attempt to steal the Ikarian virus from the Hospital Ship labs. Her husband had been sent to Ghayth on research, and she had transferred back to the *Atlas* a week earlier than he had. She was a solid performer, and from what he understood, with her new prosthetics, her hearing was now superior to normal human abilities.

Over at the bridge Science console, it was still Lieutenant Commander Karl Sheldon, who was definitely eager to get to Enki, and their First

Contact mission was his specialty too. Of course, the *Marwick* carried the RIM Confederacy First Contact team, but Tanner had been able to get his own Science officer on that team so he'd have a way to stay in the loop.

Bram Sander, his Adept officer, sat beside him on the starboard side, and as Tanner was taking stock of the crew, he turned and winked at him. Having an Issian mind reader sitting a few feet away was always a good thing. Bram smiled as he worked on something on his console monitor but that too was okay.

Tactical, of course, as on all ships, was handled by the *Atlas* XO, Commander Kondo Lazaro, Tanner's number two on the *Atlas*. Loyal, honest, with great insight—he couldn't think of a better man to have at his wing. His favorite marine, Major Alver Stal was not onboard, having taken over on Ghayth. His Air Force leader Colonel Richards was on board but down on decks where he and his pilots all had quarters and lived and worked for the most part.

In fact, other than that dang ninety days or so, things are just about the same. I'm not crazy; I'm broke but rich; I am hating tea; and the Atlas has the best crew in the Navy.

He smiled, took a big slurp of the tea, and coughed it up and all over the console. Sputtering, he got up, went over to the coffee station to get a pile of napkins, and came back to the captain's area to clean up. He grimaced. *Tea really does suck.*

Bram noted the whole thing, and he was the only one who made a comment as the rest of the bridge crew suddenly found themselves busy.

"Sir, maybe we should up that reminder note to later today," he said dryly. He smiled at least, Tanner noted, and he shook his head.

"Not at all, Lieutenant. I will give it about a month to find a home with me—or not. But the time stays firm," he said as he went back to the coffee station, tossed the big handful of wet napkins, and refilled his cup.

"Milk, maybe ..." he said to himself, and he put in a big dose of milk to try to change the taste and returned to his chair.

"Helm," he said "status on the task force, please, Lieutenant?"

Lieutenant Cooper nodded as he put the latest numbers up on the view-screen sidebar. "Sir, we're cruising at one light per day; estimated ETA is about twenty-six-plus days to this Enki planet; fuel reserves are fine; all bridge stations report all operations within range; and from the rest of the ship, we're good, Sir. Well, some kind of a minor— very minor, says CWO Hartford—snafu down in Armory Ordnance with some issues with torpedo tie-downs, but that's being handled, Sir," he said and he half-turned back to the captain.

"If torpedoes are not secure, what might happen, Lieutenant?" Tanner asked.

"Sir, as the *Atlas* has the best-latest—inertia dampeners available, even a lurch of huge size—uncommon as that might be—couldn't set one off, Sir. That's covered in classes at the Naval Academy over on Eons—first year, I believe."

Smart kid, Tanner thought. "Of course, while the torpedo would never go off—at its size of, what, sixty feet long, diameter of about four feet, she'd weigh, what, say eight tons. That's one hell of a thing to pin an Armory crewman to the walls down there, right, Lieutenant?" he said and hoped his point was made.

"Shit—sorry, Sir, I mean, yes and the chief warrant officer is looking after that—why don't I double-check on that myself, Sir?" Cooper said and his voice was contrite—almost apologetic.

Point made, Tanner thought, *and a good thing to show crewmen that the most obvious item that comes to mind can also be shown to have just as important second or more issues too.*

"Sir," Lieutenant Irving said as she half-turned to her right to see her captain, "message in from the *Marwick*—permission to put it on screen, Sir?" she said and smiled at Tanner.

He nodded and a moment later, the huge view-screen held the face of the captain of the *Marwick*.

Tanner grinned at him and said, "Aye, Captain Templeton, what can the *Atlas* do for you?"

Craig Templeton smiled at Tanner and held out his hands, palms up.

"Captain Scott, I am so sorry we can't get more speed outta this old tub—but we will get to this Enki nonetheless, Sir," he said with a hint of deprecating humor. "But we just wanted to invite you over for a real *Marwick* meal this evening— crew here just wants to pay their respects is all. Big feast has been prepared by the chefs here, and we've got Virgin Marys just for you too," he said and many of the *Atlas* bridge crew laughed.

"I accept, but only if I can bring a small group with me too—that okay, Craig?" he said which got him a big "Roger" back.

Lieutenant Irving disconnected the call and the bridge went back to normal shift duty.

As he busied himself with any starship captain's worst enemy, paperwork, he nodded to himself. *Would be good to have some of his crew bond with the Marwick folks—never can tell when one side would need backup ...*

#####

After the dinner groups had gone down to the Officers' Mess on Deck Nineteen on the *Marwick*,

Tanner and the *Marwick* captain sat alone and nursed their after-dinner coffees. Tanner had resisted—well, not really so much—asking for tea instead, and he truly enjoyed having the double-double once more. He toyed with his spoon on the napkin, moving the napkin back and forth, as he listened to Craig.

"And then, as I'm sure you can imagine, Tanner, the admiral blew a gasket. I'm not that knowledgeable about the man—but he literally stamped off cursing and went to that big bookcase behind his desk and punched a whole stack of books. Never seen him so mad—just thought that you'd want to know, is all," he said and his voice was solemn yet telling.

Tanner nodded and stared at the napkin as it slid back and forth. The admiral, it appeared, had not been happy to learn he had left the RIM Navy and had gone over to the Barony and a new captaincy on the *Atlas*.

He also knew the word on this would have come from the man he had resigned to directly—Rear Admiral Ethan Higgins had been that man on Halberd, the RIM prison planet. After quelling the prison riot and having to kill two of the rioters himself, Tanner had taken the offer from the Barony to leave the RIM Navy and take charge of the *Atlas*. It was simply a matter of considering his options and making a choice.

At least that's what he told himself, and he noted his therapy of beating his fingers on his knee one, two ... one, two was going on.

It helps, I think. , That thought sped up his fingers, but he didn't feel much more than the conscious counting of that tapping pattern ... one, two ... one, two ...

He looked up at Craig and nodded once more. "Craig, I can only imagine how he felt—in all honesty as you remember, when I left the RIM Navy, I had nothing else on my mind other than survival. You know what happened on Halberd; you were there; and you did as I did. We helped put down the riot at great cost. I would imagine that his surprise when Higgins first told him was immense, and while you were there to get your eagles, he also reminded himself of my leaving and that's just bad timing, I think. We have history too, as you know, but I'd bet that once those books stopped tumbling, he was back to all business. Right?" Tanner said and he stopped the napkin in mid-move.

Craig nodded. "Yup, got my eagles and as I rose to say my goodbyes—he simply asked if I knew why you'd resigned your commission. You know that all I could offer was a no. I really have no idea why you chose to do that—care to enlighten me too, perhaps?" he said and Tanner could hear a note of curiosity in his voice.

He really had no other reason to hem and haw so he was honest. "A few reasons, really, Craig. As you know, I had no trouble at all killing Nusayr, the leader of the whole plot to riot, and perhaps hurt some of the heads of state that where there— though I'd think the Caliph himself was his real target. It was Tibah and that flare of fanaticism in those beautiful violet eyes that she had. She looked right at me, Craig, and then aimed at the Caliph, so my navy training took over, and I killed her before her Merkel could be fired. It was the hardest shot I've ever had to take, but it had to be done. And after, I felt empty—and the thought of ever having to make that kind of a decision again was something I never ever wanted to have to do.

"The Barony offered me the captaincy of the *Atlas*, and the simple fact that I could—um—keep up my love of my Scotch with no worries. The Baroness said it plainly, and after the riot, I grabbed it. Never looked back—oh, well, I miss crew and all, but both Bram and I have fit in pretty well in the Barony Navy."

He said it and he knew it was true. He was a navy man, no doubt about it. That was the plain truth.

He took a small sip of the double-double coffee in

the mug in front of him and then shrugged. "At the same time, I know—because the shrinks all told me up on the Barony Hospital Ship—that the riot and my actions spawned my PTSD. And that was the big reason that, yes, I exploded at the bar on Neres and hurt all those Caliphate marines. How I did that, I've no idea, as I was so drunk, Craig, I remember nothing about the bar brawl. But the next ninety days up on the Hospital Ship were both boring and yet still interesting. They gave me some kind of a gene-changing shot that cured my love of Scotch—well, of all alcohol. And yes, as you can see," he said as he nodded down toward his knee at his tapping fingers, "they also gave me a combat for the PTSD. Well, not really a method to defeat it, but something that works so that when I tap that pattern over and over and over, it doesn't allow my brain to get such isolated focus on my current situation. Sort of an anti-PTSD insurance type of thing. Dunno if it works, but just talking with you now, what almost a year since the Halberd prison riots yes, has me still reacting—but not that badly. Least not so far ...

Craig reached across the table and seized his other hand.

"Captain—Tanner—I don't think you need to worry. We all knew you're sane, and while I've no idea on what those Caliphate marines said, I'm as sure as anyone else is that they deserved what they got. So you got ninety days of paid vacation, and here you are back in the captain's chair. Maybe a bit broker, rumor has it, than before but hey, next!" Craig said and he smiled at his friend.

Tanner nodded.

He wished he could explain more to his friend— about the find he'd made on Ghayth, how he felt about the Lady St. August, and the fact that even though he'd had to defend the Ikarian virus from the Caliphate too, via his killing of Jocko—but much of it was still confidential. Yet, he also knew his PTSD somehow had skipped over that event— it posed him no problem to remember and relive the exchange of fire with Jocko. No problem at all, and he noticed he was no longer tapping his fingers.

Cured! he though and smiled. *Hardly, but good to know.*

"Craig, there is more. I wanted you to know that, but I'm under big orders to yap up—but soon as I can relate those matters to you, I will. You know that I both like you and respect you—and the *Marwick* crew too. And so nice to see that you've moved up Elliot to be your XO—good choice I think too!" he said.

They grinned since they both knew finding an XO who was good for the ship as well as good for the captain could be a difficult task. Both had done so pretty well and that shared memory was a good bond between them.

"UrPoPo—should one of us mention them yet?" Craig said.

Tanner knew what he meant. As soon as the probe and its message had been received at the RIM Confederacy Council, the explosion by this member had been immense. UrPoPo believed that as this Enki world was in their system, it belonged to them to try to bring Enki aboard as one of their realm planets. Under no circumstances would they allow anyone else to "poach" on their system worlds. UrPoPo would also be attending the First Contact meetings on Enki and, they would offer— as would the RIM —the offer to join them. The UrPoPo Council member had added that they'd offer a fifty percent participation in all things rather than the much, much smaller role of being one of the hundred or so planets in the RIM Confederacy.

He looked at Craig. "I know—well, we know that the UrPoPo contingent at First Contact will be interested in one thing only. To not allow Enki to join the RIM —but to join them instead—and to be honest, Craig, I don't give a damn. But we'd surely like to know more about them and why they took, what, almost seventy years to get back to us. Talk about taking your time in making a decision ..."

#####

Standing beside his Science officer, Tanner was just plain hot. *The heat coming off the sands alone is hot enough to fry an egg. And we're the eggs,* he thought as he looked at the more than forty RIM personnel as they were led from their shuttles to the large access ramp ahead. *Couldn't we have put down a bit closer?* He sighed and nudged Lieutenant Commander Sheldon as they walked in the loose line of visitors.

"Any idea just how hot this is?" he said with a whisper. Sweat was on his upper lip, and as he spoke, little drops of that sweat were flung out and down to the hot sands below their feet.

"Sir, my PDA says its 126 degrees Fahrenheit— course, it also says it's zero percent humidity; hence we're only mildly discomforted. Well, maybe a bit more than that," he said as he too swiped the sweat off his brow.

Like most of the RIM officers, he had worn his dress blues for this First Contact meeting, and the patches of darker blue sweat discolorations were huge under his arms and all across his back. Ahead, Tanner could see the rest of the uniforms, especially the dress grays of the RIM Navy, were no longer as gray as the sweat turned them almost completely charcoal. Most of the non-military administrators were at least much lighter dressed—with a couple of their aides in simple short-sleeved shirts and pants. Even so, they too were sweating and that was to be expected, Tanner surmised, as a part of this desert planet climate.

"Thanks, Karl—and yes, it's damn hot enough," Tanner said as they slowly climbed the small set of stairs to the larger downward facing set of much bigger stairs. As they reached that vantage point, the first Enkian who had greeted them at the shuttle landing spot a couple of hundred yards away stood to one side and simply pointed downward. Earlier when they'd landed, they had gotten out assuming they were going to be entering the large pyramid that lay closest to the shuttle landing spots. They had emptied out of their shuttles and been mystified that there was no greeting party at all. They milled around and the newly appointed Enkian Ambassador had finally called for quiet as everyone argued about what to do and where to go. Instead, the man looked around and noted that a hundred feet away, standing on the sands, which were getting uncomfortably hot, a creature stood. Not a creature, he had corrected someone who'd blurted that out, but an Enkian. He slowly walked across the sands toward this native as the First Contact scenario began to play out.

Instead, the Enkian kept his distance and walked away from the big pyramid close to them and toward a large stone ramp a bit away.

Tanner had watched this Enkian either ignore or not even understand any of the initial greetings and attempts to communicate. Instead, he had simply waved his arm, which the RIM group had thought meant to follow him. They'd followed him right up to this access ramp set of stairs and now he—or she, as no one had any idea—pointed downward.

About five feet tall, the Enkian was, at least as far as Tanner could tell, an avian-based alien. While the body had no wings, other factors said so to the layperson, he thought. A crest of colored feathers ran all across the alien's head and partially down the back on its neck. While the hands looked just about normal, there were only four fingers, and the few times he'd seen the Enkian's hands, they also appeared to have larger nails—almost small talons —at the end of each digit. And the feet—two large separate toe areas again had large talon-like nails and at the back was a bigger talon-like spur that protruded, and each of the feet was covered in what looked like a scaly-type skin.

While that meant the aliens were different from humans, the colorations really stood out. The crest of feathers around the head was two different colors, a bright fire-engine red and a pure white. The head feathers were in rows of the same color, and these rows were on opposite sides of the body, which gave the Enkian a striped look. And to match that color palette, the Enkian wore a pure white robe of some type from its neck down to its knees, with again a red and white striped chest sash.

Tanner had no idea if this was normal, usual, or if this was meant to signify something to the RIM group; all he knew was the Enkian didn't have a single drop of sweat on it anywhere—none on its face or armpits or anywhere. The heat obviously didn't seem to work on an Enkian. *Wish it didn't work on us either.* He sighed to himself as he slowly went down the stairs, made of a smooth brown stone, one by one. The temperature quickly went down and down, and soon it was not quite so uncomfortable heat-wise.

It took a bit more time, but eventually the RIM group reached a large landing where the stairs spun 180 degrees, and they went down another large set of stairs. Finally reaching the bottom, they were waved at by an Enkian well ahead in the large smooth stone corridor, and they proceeded down the long corridor. The corridor was cool at least, and that was a Godsend, Tanner thought as the RIM group trooped for a few hundred yards following the corridor as it went in a slow curve to first the right and then the left. As they rounded the final curve, there were more stairs, and they sighed and began to climb them slowly.

At least, Tanner thought, *the temperature isn't rising at the same time. Maybe the Enkians used air-conditioning of some type.* The group eventually came up on a huge wide-open level, which they knew was at grade as they could see out the blue-tinged windows.

"Sir, we're on the ground floor level of that pyramid, I believe," his Science officer said as they slowly moved away from the stairwell at one end of the huge area and toward the center raised dais that held a group of Enkians all standing and waiting.

As the RIM group moved toward the waiting Enkians, they realized that all around them were Enkians in huge seated bleachers. All were seated and all with those same red and white feathers. All quiet and solemn. All waiting.

Moving toward the center raised area, the RIM ambassador took the lead, and beside him was the small translation team. As the ambassador reached the dais, he went up the three stairs to the central stage area and stopped on one side, and the translators took up a secondary spot behind him. Tanner, along with the military part of the First Contact team, moved up as well to one side and stood beside Captain Templeton and his XO too.

No one spoke. Of all the twenty or so Enkians on the stage, five stepped forward and moved to face the ambassador. None of them had wrist PDAs or any sign of a translation team either. *This is going to be interesting,* he thought as the RIM ambassador cleared his throat and took a small half step forward.

"I am Ambassador Jonathan Harmon and I represent the RIM Confederacy as we greet you for the first time."

He slightly dipped his head, perhaps to show that he deferred to them, as a small sign of respect. *I wonder if these aliens get our small gestures.* Tanner would have an answer to that question in seconds.

One of the five Enkians stepped forward too. His head feathers rippled up and down for a couple of seconds and then quieted, but they were now held upright completely on edge. His hands came around from his sides so he could clasp them in front of him. *At least I think it is a male.* One of the five was a bit shorter and had the same color feather, but those feathers were shorter and didn't stand up as much. *Female maybe,* he wondered.

The Enkian, who had fairly normal looking skin, if a bit scaly, with two eyes and a nose with nostrils that were bigger than a human's, smiled.

At least Tanner thought it was a smile, as the ends of the mouth curved upward as facial muscles were flexed.

"We are happy to have you here, Ambassador, and on behalf of the Words Muse, we welcome you to Enki—and my name is Uigoeri Qor," the alien said in what was just about perfect spoken English.

That was surprising; the ambassador tilted his head to one side and nodded. Tanner thought that for whatever reason the Enkians had learned English, it had surely been a good thing, and he smiled. The RIM group smiled and the translators were the only ones whose smiles weren't as broad. "Out of a job," Tanner said to himself and he was glad of that, as being able to communicate was what made any First Contact session a real success.

As the Enkian group of five stepped forward to meet the ambassador on an individual basis, Tanner had his eye on the rest of the Enkians and noted a couple of differences. All had the same red and white feathered crest, but some had variations on the sash that went across their chests. Instead of the red and white colored stripes, some had blue or red on tan stripes, and still others had black and lavender colors. He had no idea what any of that meant, but there were at least three types of Enkians on the stage—four if you counted the shorter one of the five heads. He turned back to listen to the ambassador ask an early question.

"May I ask a question about the use of the term 'Words Muse' and what that might mean?" he said very politely.

The shorter one of the five stepped forward, and

in a small voice, it gave what sounded like an answer, its feathered crest rippling slightly. "We suspected that this question might come to pass—so we have prepared a full presentation for you to see how our Enkian society has developed and what all of the five Muses mean. This can take some time to occur, so can you please hold that for later? Um— please would be the term, yes?" the Enkian said.

The ambassador nodded and said, "Yes, of course. Can you at least tell us how you came to learn our language? That too is of interest."

One of the other five head Enkians stepped forward and smiled again. *At least it looks like a smile.*

"Ambassador, yes, we have been studying your language now for almost seventy years—since you gave us, the Words Muse, the original offer to have us become RIM Confederacy members—which, of course, we cannot. But we did know that these talks would occur, and we knew we would have to learn English to be able to negotiate some kind of a venture to move forward. It has taken so very much time to learn and to study, and yes, we were also aided by capturing much radio and TV streaming communications from UrPoPo too. All of it helped and we hope that we do not make too many mistakes—and would ask that should that happen, you immediately correct us if possible? Would that be—okay I think you say?"

And the ambassador smiled and nodded too.

So far, Tanner thought, *this had been a pretty easy First Contact session.*

Tanner had many questions he was waiting for the answers to. Why, for instance, did Enki have no station in orbit? Where were all their Navy ships? *Wonder where the surprises are and if I'll get the answers to all my questions,* he thought as he joined the others to get closer to the Enkians and shake hands—if they did that—and looking ahead of him, he saw that, yes, they did that too.

Uigoeri Qor, head of the Words Muse, made his way back to the center of the stage the next morning, and it was easy to see that he had had one hell of a night. His feathered crest was not as big and fluffy anymore, one sign for sure. *Plus if my eyesight is still okay, there is a big stain on that sash of his, right across the red and white stripes. Odd,* Tanner thought, *but then hey, maybe he'd had syrup on his pancakes, or maybe not ...*

"I greet you and thank you for attending us here again," he said formally. Slightly behind him once again were the same four—if Tanner could even identify them—as had backed him up yesterday at the First Contact session. It hadn't taken long, and

48

they'd gone back to their shuttles to return to their ships up in orbit to wait for the next session, which was now, a day later. There had been some talk about asking if they could simply put down their ships on the sands around the Words Muse pyramid, but they had decided not to ask yet.

Tanner had taken the unexpected evening off to EYES ONLY with his favorite marine, Major Alver Stal, out on Ghayth, and they'd chatted about everything going on there. While their explorations were only about twenty percent complete, there were few signs of any more artifacts on the planet. But some odd readings were unexplainable at this point, and only further study and perhaps even some drilling would explain the readings. They commiserated about Tanner's time back on the Barony Hospital Ship and that he was barred from the OneTon bar for the future, but Alver opined that it wouldn't matter much. Any bar would work, he said and Tanner nodded even though he had his doubts. Still, good to chat and they signed off with the agreement to get together the first chance they had. Perhaps, Tanner vocalized, right after this Enki mission, and they left it at that.

He'd already had a short talk with Bram and knew that is Adept officer would be testing and checking every Enkian they met to see just how "readable" the race was. Bram looked at him and smiled, proving as usual that when Tanner thought directly about him, Bram would catch it for sure.

The ambassador and one of the administration team members took a few minutes to work out some details with the Enkians, and while they did, Tanner looked up. This pyramid was about fifty floors high, he figured, yet here in the interior, it was a soaring space way above their heads. Every so often, there were blue glass inserts all around the whole pyramid that the bright sunlight poured through but in blue tones. What could be seen from those higher vantage points was more sand. Lots of sand, and then another pyramid, and more sand and pyramids. Some of the smaller pyramids were joined together in an annex shape while still larger ones stood alone and tall. This one, called at least as far as they knew, the Words Muse pyramid, was one of the bigger ones. Tanner thought it must be air conditioned as the space within was comfortably cool.

The ambassador returned to the RIM group on the stage and waited until he had everyone's attention.

"So, we've been asked if a tour of the various different pyramids and their five muses might help us to understand what Enki is all about—and I've said yes. We will go, we will be observant, and we will ask few, if any, questions. Instead, we will await their explanations of what we are shown. We should always remember that we are guests— visitors in fact—here on Enki. So our deportment will be very polite, very civil, and we are looking for nothing to occur to be a hindrance to our discussions. Which, I've just been told, will occur next week. They have that presentation to make to us in a formal manner at this event next week. 'Til then we will get occasional tours and visits to various factors of the Enki planet. I'm told we will also get to visit what they call Resources and then their Militia too—which should make some of you Navy personnel happy! Questions?" he said and there were none.

Travel arrangements had been made, and they all trooped off the stage, down the long stairs to the curved tunnels, all the way back to the access ramp, and then up, up, and up back to the sands. There was what looked like an odd bus. It ran on more than a dozen huge inflated tires, seated up to about sixty or seventy, and was driven by an Enkian who wore the same white robe they all did but had a sash that was black and lavender striped.

"Any ideas on what the colors mean on those sashes?" Tanner asked his Science officer who had shared a seat with him.

"Sir, I did ask earlier, and that sash denotes a Resources person, or acolyte or disciple—whatever the term is—or will be. Our Words Muse folks have that red and white one. Oh, and Militia has the blue and red on tan stripes ones. What either actually means is a crapshoot, Sir. But those colors appear to be correct," Sheldon said and Tanner was glad to get the recon.

The bus moved off and after a few swings around the Words Muse pyramid, the bus accelerated and moved off toward some pyramids in the distance near the horizon. The ride was surprisingly soft on those huge inflated tires. Tanner was happy to see the driver knew about inertia and dunes and how the climb of one could often fail, so much of the ride was a big swinging curve in one direction followed by a similar one to the other side too. After almost an hour of this, the bus pulled up beside another of those access ramps, and they disembarked and took to the stairs. Down and down the stairs they went, then along corridors that reminded Tanner of tunnels through the sand, and then back up and up to the interior of that pyramid.

At the entrance they were met by more Enkians —but different ones.

These hosts were built the same as the Words Muse Enkians, but their feathered crests were of two different colors—blue and red. They had the same white robe and naked scaly feet and their sash had the same blue and red stripes. Same but different.

"Allow me," Uigoeri Qor, head of the Words Muse pyramid said, "to introduce to you the head of the Fine Arts Muse, Eecesoe Qig."

One of these new Enkians stepped forward, his feathered crest now puffed up, and the alien looked like he was very proud to have been so introduced.

"To the RIM Confederacy Ambassador and your team, we of the Fine Arts Muse would like to offer our heartfelt—is that correct—" he said to no one in particular, "welcome to our pyramid. Welcome. We have arranged for a small presentation to introduce you to our muse—would you all please follow me." Without any further discourse, he turned and left the stage, quickly moving over to the far side of this huge expanse of ground floor rotunda of their pyramid.

Against one wall, easels were setup in a long row —maybe more than three dozen of same. And on each was a canvas with some kind of a painting. Some, Tanner thought, as he got in the line to slowly pass along the row, were of real representational subjects. Enkians, pyramids, and sand dunes were some of the most common subjects. Others were abstracts of various colors, textures, and patterns. Some were very detailed, and some were cloudy like expressionism works. But all were excellent, Tanner thought, as he finished the row and then came down the back side where sculptures were also arranged in a similar row. Some were carved from the same stone as the ramps had been made from, that brown very hard stone. Others were metals, cast into shapes and forms that were somewhat representational and somewhat not so much. Again, abstracts and other unknowing styles were present, and Tanner had to admit this was great art. He thought that if he had had a full day to walk these two rows, he wouldn't have had enough time to even understand the basics of the arts he was being shown. *Not even two days,* he thought and he ended up finally joining the RIM group back on the stage. This was definitely Fine Arts, Tanner knew, and that was at least easy to understand.

After some goodbyes and the even more formal invitation from Qig, head of the Fine Arts Muse, to visit anytime—especially to attend their big monthly Arts Crawl when all the artists in the Fine Arts Muse offered up art for viewing.

Back on the bus, he looked at Bram and thought only if he'd had any luck.

"Sir, yes, Sir. From what I can tell, as a race, the Enkians know little, if anything at all, about how to 'cloud' a thought—hence yes, I can usually see what they're thinking to a degree. Sometimes, it's very, very easy—like I'm looking at a huge wall of filing cabinets, each with a small card on the front metal side of the drawer that is filled out with what lies inside. The closer to the center of where the Enkian has their focus, the easier it is to see. I can simply open the door and look inside, and that's the thinking behind whatever it is they're currently thinking about or saying. Sorry, that's a dumb metaphor, but it really is pretty easy. In fact, so easy that I can see rows and rows away of those filing cabinets to see what they thought five minutes ago or yesterday even. And to a lesser degree, I can also see what they'll be thinking and doing in five minutes and even in a few cases in an hour or more. I'm pleasantly surprised and can't for the life of me tell if my skill set has increased or if the Enkians are just very easy to read, Sir," he said and he shook his head as if the answer to that was yet unknown.

Tanner nodded. This was good to know. He now had a source to double-check whatever an Enkian told him, and reliable recon was always the best advantage to have in all things.

Then his Science officer spoke up—and he kept the volume down low too. "Sir, did you ... um ... get any of that art—so to speak?" he said.

Tanner could hear in his voice that this Science geek had looked at the same pieces he had looked at —and it meant little to him. Art was subjective, he knew, and art was not for everybody.

"Some, Karl, but not much at all. Probably an acquired taste that as yet I've not gotten either," he said and while that was probably true to a degree, still some of the art had amazed him with how he'd responded to it.

The bus wheeled around more dunes and across a huge flat wasteland of very hard-packed sand to another pyramid. The blue glass floors were bright in the sunlight, and the one they now approached was bigger than any other they'd been in. This pyramid had a set of doors right on the grade level and the bus pulled right up to the doors. There were no access down ramps, no stairs going down, and no stairs going up either. Instead, they were once again ushered into that huge pyramid ground floor rotunda, and the first thing they all noticed was the loud music playing all over the huge open space.

On stage here was another group of Enkians, but these had green and yellow feathered crests with matching colored striped sashes too.

Once more, the Words Muse head, Uigoeri Qor handled the introductions. He said, "May I now introduce Aeimeki Qir, head of the Music Muse here on Enki."

This Enkian almost seemed to strut up to meet them and half-bowed to the RIM ambassador.

Small talk ensued, and Tanner looked around the

huge space instead of listening to the niceties.

Over a few hundred feet away an orchestra—at least that's what he would have called it—played the music they were listening to right now. The conductor, Tanner noted, had an eye on the group on the stage, and someone must have signaled him as the music began to play softer and then slowly died out.

Tanner turned back to the ambassador's area, and as he did, the music began again but louder than before. He had no idea as to what the music was, but with more than one hundred live musicians on both familiar and unfamiliar instruments, played with that kind of passion, the music stirred him again. He tapped his foot at first but then stopped as the rhythms were varied and he couldn't keep up. But the melody line he loved—he learned it in less than a couple of verses, and it was enough once more for him to realize that these were professionals of a caliber he'd never before experienced.

That thought alone carried him through the next two pyramids, and before he even entered them, he knew he would be more than impressed.

At the Dance Muse pyramid, with Enkians who had gray and brown feather colorations, he was enthralled with the lyrical dance that was a full forty-minute presentation. The way these Enkians moved and how they were able to pass on feelings and emotions that he was able to not only "get" but understand too was mind-boggling. *And I'm an alien to them and their culture ... what must these arts do to Enkians would be the real question.*

At their final pyramid, Performance Muse, the Enkians with their purple- and orange-feathered crests and sashes treated the RIM group to a full two-act play. The story was about an Enkian from one muse pyramid who fell in love with an Enkian from another muse pyramid and the issues they faced. *Love does conquer all, it seemed, no matter whether a human or an alien. And that's exactly what this play presented.*

On the way back to the Words Muse pyramid, there were many conversations among the RIM group, and their Enkian hosts chimed in with answers where needed.

Enki, they said, was made up of the five muses — Words, Dance, Music, Performance, and Fine Arts. Each had hundreds of pyramids all around the planet. Each had their own followers who lived, breathed, and died with their muse. Each had no time or interest in the other muses. Each was charged with the duty to follow their muse with passion and to make it the most important part of their lives.

But yes, there were often difficulties. Some

Enkians tried to surpass their limitations, and that's what the Militia was all about. Raised to be completely honest and uncaring about any of the muses, their jobs were to follow the orders of the jurors—the ruling judicial power on Enki and to enforce the laws and judgments of the jurors. Each pyramid had a Militia stationed within it to help the local muse council run the pyramid.

The Resources group was another equally important group. *These are the geeks and nerds as we call them,* Tanner thought. The Resources group was responsible for the technology, the mining, and the manufacturing on the planet, as well as the agriculture in those areas of Enki where things would grow.

One of the administrators said nicely, "Mr. Ambassador, it's like the arts run the world and everyone else just isn't so important. They do the bidding of each of the muses—well, unless something is sent to these jurors for a trial perhaps?"

One of the Words Muse leaders nodded and leaned forward, his finger with that small talon nail pointing directly at that RIM administration man.

"That is a concise way to describe what we are, what we do and yes, how any issues are decided. Then I would think that this tour was a success— we thought it better to show than to tell our RIM ambassador about what Enki is all about," he said and there were looks of satisfaction among the Enkians on the bus. *Well, looks of satisfaction if rippling feathered crests counted for anything.* Tanner recalled the paintings he'd seen in the Fine Arts Muse pyramid. *Wonder how someone could buy one of those...* He noodled this around in his brain and decided he'd ask about that as soon as he could

CHAPTER TWO

In one of the smaller annex pyramids, located next to but still attached to the Fine Arts Muse pyramid, a meeting of the Enkian leadership was in full swing. In a small conference room, more than seven of them were arguing and the topic was the RIM Confederacy.

"That is just something we should consider," Eecesoe Qig said, trying to make his point that they would be foolish to ever be honest with these aliens. While he was the leader of the Fine Arts Muse, he could not order the rest of them to follow his lead.

That got a few heads nodding, and yet others present disagreed.

"I do not think that you have considered all of the various items that we've learned about this Confederacy. We have been studying them for over seventy years, and from what we know, they are a well-run democracy-styled society. All they want is for us to join—and as Words has the lead on this—we do not have a vote on that. Only the Words Muse can do that for all of Enki."

Around the table, more heads nodded. Each of the Enkians was involved in this discussion because each of them was a department head.

Each was responsible for the future in their own area for their muse citizens.

And each was fed up with the fact that Words would be the controlling muse for the whole RIM membership.

Words Muse had followed the Fine Arts Muse orders of over fifty years ago and had sent the message to the RIM Confederacy. It was that message that had brought this RIM group to them to offer up membership in the Confederacy. And it was that feeling of being personally involved with this that was the sore point for most of them at the table.

Some, however, felt that it was Words' job to do as they were ordered to do—and to do no more. But that was not the consensus at the table.

"We need to be honest with the aliens, but we do not need to tell the RIM ambassador or anyone in that group what we are planning. Do we at least agree on that?" one said and that received more nods—but again not all around the table.

"Not seeing it," some said and few supported that feeling.

No consensus meant little would be done, everyone knew ... and that's how it looked to each of them.

Down three floors underground, in a small laboratory tucked off one of the wings of the Naval Base technology building, three scientists in white lab coats were staring up at a large display screen. They were looking at a spreadsheet full of numbers and macros that made long formulas appear in the proper cells.

"Andre, are we absolutely sure that the formulas are exact?" one said.

Andre smiled and clicked a couple of keys on the keyboard in front of him, and the spreadsheet compressed as a lengthy formula came on screen. He scrolled it down to the bottom of the text box and then back up to the top.

"You can certainly double-check my entry—but yes, it's exact," he said. A few key presses made the formula disappear, and the spreadsheet took over the same full-screen display.

"The numbers do not lie. This metal—more than three hundred square feet of it from the Enki probe

—is an element we do not know. It appears to be inserted somewhere in the table of elements as HREE bound—but somehow it has some yttrium or lanthanide's factors. No matter at this point, as we begin more tests later today. But at this point, the numbers above show, that it has—or may have as testing will either prove or disprove, some interesting features. One of which we think might be a toughness factor that we at this point can't measure. But testing will give us some ideas," Andre said as they all stared up at the numbers.

The scientists continued to stare up at the spreadsheet and ponder the numbers that were there.

"Testing. What kind of testing are we doing, Andre," the same scientist asked.

"Standard stuff for new elements—not that we have a standard group of tests. We'll use Atomic Emission Spectroscopy or AES, ICP-MS Analysis, Carbon and Sulfur Determination, Energy Dispersive X-ray Spectroscopy or EDS, and Gravimetric and Volumetric Wet Chemistry Analyses too. You know, the full gamut and hopefully we can determine exactly what it is," Andre said.

"It sure cuts easily, though," one of them said and he was right. The automatic shearing machine had made easy work of cutting smaller ten-foot-by-ten-foot panels.

The one scientist who'd been asking the questions offered up one more. "Can we test something else too? Can we use a full set of Projectile and Ray tests too?" he said.

Andre raised an eyebrow and nodded. "Done, and the results will be available in a few hours," he said as he typed in the extra tests and they were done for now.

#####

The Words Muse pyramid, like all the Enkian pyramids, was a complete city within a series of attached pyramids. In this muse, there were five interconnected pyramids. One was taller than the rest, and the leaders of the Words Muse met here daily. While the other smaller pyramids were mostly a collection of citizen apartments or common areas like cafeterias, games rooms, or lounges, the main function of the largest pyramid was to house and showcase their muse. Many of the lower floors held writers lounges and playwrights workshop rooms. Then there were the editing studios where those who wrote the lyrics for songs or words for show tunes worked daily. There were also larger presentation rooms where authors read their manuscripts, chefs compared their recipes, and other Words Muse citizens held small shows and performances to display their work.

The biggest presentations made by Words Muse citizens were held in the huge ground floor rotunda area, which was also used by the jurors. Here, the jurors presided over any of the cases and trials the Words Muse had on the dockets. Now there were only a couple of minor cases and trials pending.

The main pyramid was tall, more than a thousand feet from the base to the very top. At the very top of the Words Muse pyramid was a room that only the leaders had access to. At the door stood a brace of Militia guards, who made sure to have each of the five leaders check in with them before gaining access to the room. Inside the room was a simple round table with five uncomfortable chairs. While that didn't make their meetings much shorter, it did make them all shift and squirm just as they were doing right now.

Uigoeri Qor slapped the table once more to get some kind of order and the other four quieted down.

"Look, I know we have similar thinking on this— but what is it we might be missing? What is it we need to consider to help our cause? Ideas, please?"

Everyone started talking at the same time once more. He sighed and slapped the table once more, then again, and again. He looked to his immediate left and nodded to the Enkian beside him.

"Uugredi, please … you begin. And I would ask
that the rest of you stay quiet until he is done,"
Uigoeri said and he slapped the table to ensure that
at the least they knew he was going to try to ensure
each would have a turn to speak. His beak cracked
as he slammed it down a few times to emphasize
his point.

"Uigoeri, thank you for starting with me—and
yes, as you all know, I along with Uangriu, we run
the muse here at Words. Our work is ongoing and
yes, lengthy, and all encompassing. But what I have
to say does not cover the muse itself—instead, I
want to speak to what it is we want to do as a
whole," he said as his feathered crest rippled and
then lay down, an Enkian sign of importance. He
shifted in his seat and then leaned forward to look
at all of them around the table, his beak chattering
slightly.

"We face a major opportunity here, to put a
Words Muse male—yes, I mean Uigoeri here—into
the opening up leadership of the jurors. As we
know, the current leader, Iavoesi Qax, will leave
office in just a month. He has made it well known
that he will endorse no one—so we must take that
as an opportunity to fill that position with our own
leader. We agree there, I believe, completely within
this room," he said and that did get several nods.

"So, using the RIM Confederacy to help us do

that—is not only taking advantage of the opportunity that their current membership offer brings us—but as we know, we can parlay that and be successful. Uigoeri will be the next head juror is the answer. Our answer," he said and that got more nods.

Uanstard Qor, the Words Muse Enkian who looked after the Militia, butted in. "And, as we all know, we have the muscle to push this through. Yes, we are taking advantage of an opportunity of using the RIM Confederacy to gain our own ends —but that's what opportunity is—and we have it right now," he finished off and slapped the table in front of him.

Uigoeri smiled and held up his hand to stop them. He was one of the few Enkians who used a light polish on his hand talons, and it shone now in the late afternoon light that flowed into the room. While the windows were the same blue as was used everywhere else on the pyramid, up here they were a deeper hue as the windows were much thicker.

Uigoeri nodded, looked down at the Agenda in front of him, and half-smiled at the list. "We appear to be running a bit behind on our timeline—but we at least have one item fully considered and done. Next is the request from Resources for more workers from the reserves to handle the increase of the new younglings and their care. Ustepori, please?" he said and the Resources manager here in the Words Muse stood to present his report.

The latest large increase in the younglings and their much-underestimated numbers meant that the staff down in the Resources incubator wards was overpowered. As everyone knew, care of an Enkian began as soon as the eggs were gathered and then put into the incubators. Monitoring of the year-class was a twenty-four-seven job, and when the eggs hatched, each youngling had to be enrolled into the Words Muse, IDs recorded, files created, and vitals taken every day. It was a long, tedious, and difficult job, and Resources needed more help. "Plain and simple," Ustepori said and he sat.

Discussion ensued and they all agreed they would need to up their level of Resources to cover those new helpers and yes, increase their budgets accordingly. This was not a happy answer, Uigoeri knew, but it was something that happened every few years when the egg numbers increased for what appeared to be no known reason. "Younglings," he said to himself, "were always an issue." For a moment, he wondered if any might be his own and then shrugged it off ... what did it matter, they were just younglings.

One day, one of them might sit here in my chair, but not today.

Desert Planet

Bram sat quietly on his bed—he usually referred to it as a bunk because on a frigate or cruiser, that's what it was. But on the *Atlas*, he had such a large private quarters apartment, that instead of this being a bunk, it was a full queen-sized bed with a headboard that held books and a nightlight he often used often to read by late at night. Beside him, on the bed covers, he had an opened copy of his latest read, something from a long, long time ago about beheadings of kings and the like in a place called France. *Wonder where that planet even is? Gotta remember to Gallipedia that too later.*

But now, it's time to go to Eons—well so to speak.

It no longer hit him as hard as it had years ago; instead, that cavernous black hole suddenly grew up around him like a fog.

He knew as his hands suddenly grabbed at the edge of the bed just under his legs that they usually did just this, but again he couldn't even feel the bed.

He could see nothing. He could hear nothing. He knew not to succumb to the nausea; while he no longer vomited when this happened, it was only because he was able to quell that reaction and response. He simply fell and waited.

In front of his eyes, the pinpoint of light suddenly popped into being, and as that tiny spotlight grew to a brighter and brighter larger ball of light, it was to be expected. He used to be so scared when this happened but not any longer.

He could hear the whispers too all of a sudden, as they intertwined and linked and built on each other until they were no longer whispers but shouts and shrieks, and again, as usual, one shout seemed to be louder and take over as the others faded. As it came to the forefront, its volume level was reduced and then it turned into a voice. A voice he knew and trusted. A voice that somehow seemed familiar ...

The Master Adept appeared directly in front of him as the blackness around him snapped out of existence and his quarters appeared to his now working eyes.

"Once again, Adept Sander, we are mind-linked and we welcome you.

As she said that, more Adepts popped into view around him. Eight, nine, no, there were ten of them now including the Master who were also mind-linking with him. Here but not really here. Just here in his mind.

He nodded to them and said out loud, "Welcome, Master ... welcome, all," as he looked from one face to another.

On Eons, dozens of light years away, the Master straightened up in her chair, leaned forward to the linked Adepts, and spoke to them all.

"You will know, of course, that Adept Sander is on Enki—the latest candidate planet to join our RIM Confederacy. While that is one thing that we are unconcerned with, normally, in this case it's the point of our mind-link today," she said and stopped.

It was as if, Bram thought, *she needed some time to frame the issue in her own mind maybe.*

Or maybe she just needed to burp, he also thought, and that brought a smile to his face, which he quickly wiped away.

She looked at the group once again and again leaned forward. "What the problem is—and I know a few of you here with long-standing skills already know—is that we are facing an issue here on the RIM that is perilous for our continued longevity. I mean that while we few cannot as yet identify the exact cause, what we see is a major crux approaching. One that we want, of course, to go our own way—to prevent what we also see as war on the RIM."

That got a gasp from some on the mind-link and from Bram too.

"We know little. But what we do know is that the Enki candidacy is important to this, but we do not know how. So I now invite you to contribute—to see what we can as a group come up with consensus-wise to help. And Adept Bram will be the Adept on the spot too ..."

Bram listened as some of the Adepts asked more questions, but it was apparent there was little more factual evidence that the Master had for them. Some of the other Adepts offered that if Enki became a RIM Confederacy member, that might be the cause of this unknown war—and perhaps that should be addressed. But a few others said nonsense to that and the group as a whole was divided.

The Master looked at them and waited, and no one offered up anything more, so Bram decided now was his time.

"Master and Adepts, I have something to add to this too, if I may?"

The Master simply nodded.

Bram leaned forward too and tried to explain what he had found out about the Enkians as a race and how he had tried his abilities out with them. They were all surprised at how easy he claimed they were to read—and even more surprised that as a young Adept officer, he was able to even see their futures to a lesser degree. Some had questions and more than one liked his metaphor of the walls of filing cabinets, each with a little card on the drawer telling what was inside. They asked more questions, and he had to admit that he really didn't know if the males were easier than the females or the mature easier than the younglings. In fact, he had to offer that he saw them as all the same—there was no difference that he could tell. One, the Adept who was from the moon of Eons, Tavira was the city there, offered up one more thing, and that was interesting, Bram thought.

"Have you tried our input test, Bram?" she asked and they all sat to hear the answer.

The input test was a difficult thing to attempt, Bram knew from his years on Eons, but one that he'd never tried before. Basically, it was the test where an Adept Issian would try to input into a subject's brain—sort of opening up a filing cabinet door, replacing whatever was there with a thought of your own, and then writing the idea down on the little card for that drawer. It was said that this took years—decades perhaps—of effort to increase their skills for the Adepts who attempted this with success. And the thought to even try this was a new one for him.

"Yes, good point, Adept Octavia—Bram you are hereby charged with that duty. Please pick an easy item—nothing that would be against the Enkian sense of morality or religious or political issues. Make it small. Make it easy for you to tell the difference and report back via EYES ONLY soonest. I want to know if that might be a possibility for us too. Best of luck, Bram," she said as the room full of the rest of Adepts all faded and he was alone with the Master

She nodded to him. "Bram, you are the Adept on the Enkian scene, so you need to rise to this occasion. You can EYES ONLY me any time on this matter, but we need to know the results of the input test soonest, Bram," she said and then she smiled at him.

As she faded out, her mind said to his mind, "And Bram, if I need to burp, I just do that on its own ..." and she was gone.

He smiled. *If I can do this, that might actually help us, and that's a good thing, and if not, then back to the drawing board ...*

Tanner and Bram, his Adept officer who obviously didn't see this coming, were stopped at the fringe of the huge Words Muse pyramid ground floor rotunda and taken aside by a Militia officer. Tanner studied the man in the camouflage uniform. While the name-tag was there, there were some service stripes he thought on one arm and a badge he didn't recognize in the uniform collar.

"Sir," he said politely, "I do not know your rank — could you enlighten me, please?" he said as he half-pointed at what looked like some kind of an armadillo-type armored animal.

"Yes, it's a stonecraw — a desert animal that we have all over the planet. The rank is about equal to what would be a lieutenant, and I'm a first class stonecraw — Stonecraw Qew, Sir, an enlisted NCO rank, that is, Sir," he said, and he smiled at Tanner.

"Pleased to meet you, StoneCraw Qew — is that the correct usage?" Bram asked and that got a nod back to him.

"Sir, yes, Sir. And might I add that we are very up-to-date with your background, Captain — we received the full dossier on all the members of the RIM group as a matter of course. They were supplied by your own RIM Confederacy Executive Council, we were told — and reading about your past was the most interesting read in the whole package. Sir," he said, and he snapped to attention and saluted as the Militia did on Enki. Both hands, heart high and palms facing down, were slapped against his chest and held for about five seconds or so, and then he relaxed.

Tanner nodded. There was nothing else to say.

Tanner and Bram had been intercepted so they could be seated away from the rest of the RIM group of visitors. StoneCraw Qew, escorted them off to one side, and they climbed about a dozen of the rows of seats, took their reserved seats, and smiled at all the camouflaged Enkians who surrounded them.

"Seems like we're with the Enki Militia, Sir," Bram said and that got a nod of agreement.

Below on the floor in a large floor seating area, the RIM ambassador and most of the rest of the group were already seated. Tanner noted that Captain Templeton didn't appear to be there, and he scoured the rest of the bleacher seats across from them first, then beside them, and yes, there they were. They, like Bram and he, were seated with more Militia rows, and that seemed odd for a moment. But there were many more present, Tanner could see. More than a few thousand, Tanner thought, and yet for that many Enkians, the overall noise level was not too much to bear.

"Maybe, they just thought that we soldiers need to sit with soldiers—rather than with the ... the ... politicians, I'd say," Bram said, and Tanner snickered.

"Here I am," he said to himself, "turning forty years of age in a few short weeks. I've been a military man—navy man that is, since I went to the Earldom of Kinross Academy more than twenty years ago. Black hair except for a hint of some gray at the temples. Blue eyes, but they have seen much and some of that had been plainly life changing. I have never been truly—completely—in love with a woman except maybe for the Lady St. August, but that is still too new to know." His fingers tapped on

77

his knee, one, two ... one, two, and then there had
been Tibah, but that was over. One, two ... one, two
...

"Sir", Bram said as he nudged his elbow into
Tanners side a bit more abruptly than needed,
"looks like the jurors are coming in ..."

That interruption took Tanner's attention away
from Tibah and the prison riot, and his fingers
gripped his knee as he turned to his left to watch
the procession.

Jurors, they'd been told, were the uppermost
judicial body on Enki. It was their job—similar to
the Supreme Court on any planet, he thought—to
decide major cases and call them the way they saw
them for all Enkians. While the basics were perhaps
similar on all planets, he doubted they were the
same on all. *My own Barony had, yes, the Appellate
Court—who took their marching orders from the
Baroness.* He smiled and wondered if it was the
same on all planets with Royals.

From the left side of the rotunda, there was a
slow procession of about a dozen Militia, but it was
too far away for Tanner to see their ranks, and if the
stonecraws came in first. Moving like a drill, the
two columns marched all in step, their heels loudly
clicking on the stone floor. The first few mounted
the steps, and then they all came to a halt, turned to
face the other column, and came to attention.

Moments later at a command from the drill leader, they saluted and that too was different. Instead of using one hand to point to their head using the eyebrow as a guide—the Enkian Militia used something different. Both hands moved to the chest and both hands were palm down toward the floor. The men held that pose and then Tanner noted another thing. Instead of their feathered crests standing up tall or ruffling, they laid down those feathers as flat as possible and held them immobile.

From the same entrance below and to the left, five Enkians now walked out in single file. Each was a juror, Tanner knew, as they were dressed like all Enkians in that white robe—but their feathers were the green and yellow of jurors only. No other Enkians had that coloration and that made Tanner think about how that was done, but that'd be for a later conversation. The jurors walked along between the twin rows of saluting Militia, mounted the stage, and took their seats at the table. The twin rows of Militia fell out of formation and took seats in the front row in front of the bleachers Tanner was seated in.

Iavoesi Qax, the head juror, rose after a moment and that quieted the huge area quickly.

He looked around the room and then down at the RIM group who were seated close to the stage.

"We were asked by the Words Muse to hold this

presentation on behalf of the whole Enkian planet, and we have agreed to represent the judiciary here as asked. To speak today to the RIM ambassador, may I present Uigoeri Qor, leader of the Words Muse here on Enki," he said, and from the left side, a single Enkian walked out and toward the stage. Moments later, he mounted the dais and turned his back on the jurors to face the seated RIM group just in front of him.

He seemed to gather himself and looked around at the seated crowd around him first.

And then, he faced the RIM group.

"We, first, would like to thank the RIM Confederacy for their quick response to our offer made and sent to them, almost sixty years ago. And that is what we should address first. We do not have the technology that exists here in the RIM or, for that matter, probably all across the galaxy. We do not have FTL —as you all know, it took one of our speediest probes more than fifty-five years for it to go from Enki to Juno. And the RIM came here in less than a month. We also understand that there is something called the Ansible—a device that can let someone communicate with anyone anywhere in real time. We wonder what it might be like to have those kinds of technology devices here in Enki, and yet they are not so important to us. We are a very closed-off society; we value the muses too much, we feel, to ever need such devices or what they might bring to us. We enjoy our solitude, and yet, we know that we should face change as it occurs. It is the way of progress, and we have learned to accept that change but at our own speed," he said and that comment got a thousand beaks clacking.

Must be what we call applause, Tanner thought, and he waited for it to slow.

The head of the Words Muse waited too, and finally with a ripple of his feathered crest, the clacking stopped.

"We want you, Mr. Ambassador, to understand what happened here on Enki when your initial request for us to join the RIM Confederacy was received. It—as I'm sure you now understand— prompted a trial between us—Words Muse and the Performance Muse. They argued that as the offer to join the RIM came as a video, it was a performance; hence the offer was made to them. We argued, more successfully it appears, that the performance—the video—was a simple reading of the words that were on the single document delivered to Enki. We won," he said and that got the beaks clacking a bit, but they died down quickly. "And so the decision to join the RIM Confederacy will be ours alone to weigh and consider and then make our decision."

With that, he half-turned and held out a hand to the jurors behind him.

The clacking started once again, and it lasted for a few minutes.

Rising from his seat, the head juror, Iavoesi Qax, nodded, and then his feathered crest ripple stopped the clacking.

"I wanted to let you—the RIM Ambassador and all of your group—know that yes, the decision for our planet is in the hands of the Words Muse, as they were the ones that you approached. The decision will be theirs, and it will occur soon, we are told," he finished off.

Tanner thought he sounded like he had no idea. *Figures that the politicians and administrators and the whole civil service would have no idea at all.*

He smiled and the RIM ambassador rose in the crowd. Qor noticed and his rippled feathered crest stopped the crowd's noise immediately.

"We would just like to thank the jurors and the Words Muse too, their leaders and their citizens, for their consideration of our offer. As soon as we have a chance to work out the details and come to a working deal, we will Ansible back our deal to the RIM Confederacy for their final decision."

There was neither a single clack nor a rippled feathered crest in the room.

Oh-oh, Tanner thought, *what's up with that?*

Uigoeri Qor, the head of the Words Muse, took a step back, and his beak was wide open. All the jurors behind him looked the same and that, as far as Tanner could tell, was Enkian for "what the hell?"

A moment later, Qor took another step forward and nodded.

"Then I take it, Mr. Ambassador, that you are not a decision maker—but simply a messenger. You cannot speak on behalf of the RIM at all—and if that is true, then it appears that we were under the wrong impression. Is that true, Ambassador?" he said, and again there was no noise at all in the huge rotunda.

Ambassador Harmon nodded at first. Then he looked beyond the Words Muse leader to the head juror seated behind him.

"Just as in your society, where a muse can do as it pleases and then the jurors have to carefully measure and decide—we too in the RIM Confederacy do the same thing. It is our job to make the best deal we can for the RIM —and then it goes back to our own 'jurors' for their confirmation. We are very similar, Qor, and that is the plain truth of the matter," Harmon said, and Tanner knew he'd just heard a master spin on this.

Qor stared at him. He took a half step backward and then forward. His feathered crest rippled, and all the beaks in the room were all clacking at once.

The din was major and Tanner and Bram, along

with most of the RIM group, clapped their hands.

"Point made and point taken," Tanner said to himself, and the clacking and clapping went on for quite a while.

#####

On the bridge of the *Atlas*, Tanner was surprised to see he had a request for a private Ansible from Ambassador Harmon, which he immediately accepted but moved over to his captain's ready room off to one side of the bridge.

Been here not so often, he thought, as he carefully set down the cup of green tea on his desk. Not bad tea—not as good as his double-doubles of coffee—but with two milks and two sugars, it was close to being palatable. One of the *Atlas* stewards had commented that it was so close to what he used to have, he might as well just go back to the coffee. "Man was right though," he said to himself, and he snorted his displeasure at being called out.

Coffee ... tea ... it didn't matter what he had, as long as it was a virgin pick-me-up. No Scotch included was the mantra to bear.

He sat and then clicked the button on the keyboard. The monitor came on with a RIM Confederacy seal in the center. Moments later, it faded to black, and then the face of Ambassador Harmon came on screen.

He looks somewhat off, Tanner thought. *Maybe it's the collar of his shirt that was a bit bent out of shape. Maybe it's his one hand tapping a pencil on the desk he is at over on the Marwick. Maybe it's the way he glanced down at what looked like a paper in front of him.* Tanner had no real idea, but something was up.

"Mr. Ambassador, how can I help you?" he said and sipped his tea, enjoying the mouthful of the milky, sweet hot liquid.

Harmon nodded first. Then he looked like he was trying to find an answer. All of which, Tanner knew, meant that this "master of spin" had as yet not gotten a handle on what to say.

"Captain Scott, I am asking to speak to you for a very specific reason—one that I'd like to keep confidential. Do we understand each other, Captain?"

Tanner nodded and that seemed to work for the ambassador.

"Captain, something, well, something unusual has happened. I was contacted by one of the other muses down on Enki—the Fine Arts Muse—and they have made an interesting proposition to us— well, to the RIM Confederacy, I mean. And this is a clandestine conversation and an offer—but one that we are to keep to ourselves. I was approached myself when I was with Captain Templeton of the *Marwick,* and we both were whisked away to a small room off the rotunda, and we heard their request. And it was Captain Templeton who suggested that we bring you in on this as he says you have great experience with military forces; your past, he relayed to me, includes more than our own RIM or Barony Navy," he said. He looked down at that paper in front of him.

Tanner waited.

No interruptions.

He knew that often, if you just wait, you get more information than the other side wanted to offer.

Ambassador Harmon continued. "I have made some notes, Captain Scott, but I believe that it boils down to this. Fine Arts says that the head juror— this Iavoesi Qax—will be retiring in about a month. The job of head juror is the most prized position on the planet, and the head of the Words Muse— Uigoeri Qor—is running in the election for that job. He's the front-runner, they tell me, and it is expected that if he wins, things will become more hard-nosed conservative here on Enki. And that has them worried. What they have proposed—if that is even the term for this—is that if we support publicly their own leader—Eecesoe Qig—for the head juror position, they will ensure that Enki accepts the RIM Confederacy offer. No matter what Words Muse decides on our offer, they would challenge that decision, and it would go to the jurors for their final judicial decision, and as their man is now the head juror, case closed," he said, his voice very much matter-of-fact.

Tanner wondered, first of all, if this was how the diplomatic dealings were handled when it came to the civil service. Deals that were made in back rooms just like this one were never known and therefore never suspect either.

Next was the thought that perhaps this Fine Arts Muse contact was lying—that they had other hidden agendas in all of this.

Or, they could be being led down a path that would ensure there would never be a deal between the RIM and Enki.

Most of all, I'm just glad I have nothing to do with all of this—except, it appeared to offer up some counsel. So here goes ...

"Ambassador, there are so many unknowns and variables here, I couldn't possibly make a value judgment here that could help. As Craig said, my experience is in the military—the navy world. That I know. And that's all that I know, Sir," he said, and he hoped that the honesty he felt had been carried by his voice.

The ambassador nodded and sat quietly for a moment. "All right, Captain. Here's what I know you can do that would help. What I'd like for you to do—and I'll arrange this on your behalf—would be for you to tour as much of the Enki Militia areas that you can. I want a report, EYES ONLY to me daily, on what you've found, what their military strength is and would or could be, and maybe more importantly, I want to know about their personnel. In every area, from officers down to enlisted men and women. I want to have a comprehensive and detailed report on what kind of forces the RIM might face, if this all goes south. And I want a complete poll of their military technology too, from sidearms to plasma cannons and whatever they might have in between. Understood, Captain?" he said, and Tanner could almost feel the steel in that question.

"Absolutely, Ambassador. If you can arrange those trips and visits, then my reports will be on your console the next day, Sir," he said.

"Done, Captain. And as a side note, while I was not on Halberd during that whole prison riot, I just wanted to say thank you for your more than adequate defense of the RIM heads of state. Your actions were exemplary and I thought worth more than just a thank you. Well done, Sir," he said, and Tanner heard the honesty in his voice.

As the console monitor screen faded to black, Tanner sat back and sipped his tea. It was cold now, but the sweetness was still good. *Green tea, that is my new double-double, and that's the end of that story.*

This whole behind-the-scenes covert stuff is a situation that is going to be interesting. At least I'll see some of the planet and their various bases, he thought. "That's always a good thing, right?" he said to himself and yet knew there was really no answer that would work.

CHAPTER THREE

"Final set of Ray tests," the research lab assistant said as he added in the day's date and time and the lab location. Not that the real location of the lab was really used, as this large laboratory was five floors underground in the technology building on the Neres Naval Base grounds. They used the same surrogate lab locations all the time, so anyone who knew that knew this lab was the most secure, best protected, and most difficult to gain entry to of all the labs.

Still, the lab assistant thought, *it wouldn't take a genius to break that dumb subterfuge,* and he chuckled.

He was still somewhat amazed, though, that the results of the previous three days' testing, when sent up the hierarchy chain of the Science Ministry, had not produced more suits down here. Of course, the Projectile testing had been as expected. Sidearm bullets bent and twisted the metal; the Merkel carbine loads had pierced it easily, so they had called off any larger projectile testing. As all metals, the thickness of the metal had to be taken into account for any kind of stopping of a projectile.

Maybe they're all in meetings or in a mess somewhere having cheap beers. No matter, the tests so far today should get some reaction.

But as always—this he knew innately—*I must ensure that the tests are all perfect in their parameters and standards.* He sighed loudly and went over to the test console, and using his thumb, he signed in.

The test parameters form came right up, and he keyed in the proper items and ensured all the necessary fields were filled in properly. The test lab AI was pretty good, he knew, but the eyes of a live person were always the final security check that was expected. *And today*, he thought, *they'd double-check his work a hundred times, looking for the barest hint of an error. But not today.*

He went over to the isolation test room window and took a good look—a study really of what lay inside.

One wall held the various delivery mechanisms for the rays that they'd be testing. There were others too, of course. Yesterday, they'd used the Projectile magazines, to speed various types of cartridges and other items into the large ten-foot-by-ten-foot sheet of the Enkian metal that was suspended in the center of the isolation room. Today the Ray nozzles would be used, for plasma, laser, and energy pulse weapons.

Today will finish the final run of tests.

Tomorrow the you-know-what hits the fan.

He smiled, went back to the console, and chose the last remaining items.

Plasma nozzle settings included temperature—*check*, ion cyclotron radiation—*check*, and Thomson scattering levels. *All check.*

Energy pulse settings were fewer, but he ensured the electric resistance levels were well within their recommended range. *Check.*

Lasers were even easier, as he let the AI program a normal spread, volume, and varieties of gas, sapphire and excimers too. *Check.*

All the variations were covered; all the ranges tested and true.

Time to push the button, he thought, and he went off to the right, out of the big lab into the secure control room, and he put on the lead-shielded long vest, his eyewear, and the headphones too and went to stand in front of the view monitor.

A big countdown timer appeared in the view-screen sidebar, and when it reached 3-2-1, he flinched. He knew he was safe, he knew the rays were all aimed at the Enkian sheet of metal from their probe, yet he couldn't help it.

Plasma first—and the flares were huge. Normally in outer space, this weapon had a viable range of over 10,000 miles—today it was going all of twenty feet.

The colors were bright. Thanks to the glasses, he was able to see the green ray itself as it struck the Enkian metal sheet.

He knew, as did every Navy man, that a plasma weapon was a type of weapon that fired a stream or toroid of plasma—very hot, very energetic excited matter. The primary damage mechanism of this weapon was usually thermal transfer; it typically caused serious burns, and often immediate death of living creatures, and melts or evaporates other materials. Yet here, the ray was trained directly on the metal sheet, about twenty feet away, and nothing happened. He clicked the over-ride toggle switch on the control panel in front of him and let the plasma rain down on the metal for more than thirty seconds. No damage. Not a bit and as his eyes opened up even more, he looked at the sidebar and noted the temperature sensors reported no noticeable change in the metal at all. Nothing. Plasma weapons were unable to destroy the metal, and the temperature remained the same.

His eyes widened at that short unscientific

summation, but he realized the suits upstairs would be jumping up and down.

He watched the rest of the tests too—the Energy Pulse weapon resulted in no change to the metal. The tests used wide-ranging mass, power, density, or particle/energy density coefficients, and not a single noticeable change was made to the metal sheet from Enki. "Not a one," he said to himself, "and now the lasers."

He half-closed his eyes once more, even though he was protected. Laser weapons moved at the speed of light, no matter what type of laser was the underlying source. The laser tried first to drill into the metal, to no avail. Then the laser was moved in a pattern to see if the movement of the light might work, and again, nothing happened. Finally, the laser used higher and higher frequency modulation —and still no damage to the sheet of metal.

The laser snapped off and the lab assistant looked up at the sidebar on the vitals of that sheet of metal.

Not a single factor had changed. Temperature, tensile strength, atomic absorption, inductive coupling, magnaflux indicators—all the vital factors were there. And once again, the Enkian metal had come through the testing fine.

The metal appeared to be invulnerable. Not a single weapon had caused any kind of metal breakdown at all, projectile or ray.

He smiled. . He left the secure control room and returned to the larger lab itself.

Tomorrow ...

#####

The console at the captain's console on the bridge of the *Atlas* chimed three times. It appeared, Tanner thought, as he looked down at the monitor, that he was receiving a call from Enki, from the Words Muse pyramid. A personal message had been sent to him and that was unusual. Also, there was no name in the field where the sender should have been listed.

"This is Captain Scott. Who am I speaking to?" he said as his finger tapped the accept button.

A voice he thought he recognized came through the speaker to him.

"Sir, this is Stonecraw Qew—we met just a day or two ago at the Words Muse presentation—do you remember me, Sir?"

Tanner was surprised but he remembered the soldier.

"Yes, yes, I do remember you, Stonecraw. And what can I do for you today?" he asked, and he wondered to what he owed this pleasure.

"Sir, long story—but the meat of same is that you've been granted some kind of 'special envoy' status with the Militia. And my own colonel asked if anyone in our group knew you personally. I answered not really but that was like taking a step forward, Sir. So I've been assigned the job of being your official escort for your upcoming list of visits to various Militia bases and operation centers. Sir."

He jammed a lot of information into those few sentences, but Tanner got the gist of the story. *Seems like the ambassador had already made some distance in his quest to get me some military visits.*

"Stonecraw, I got it. And I like it. I think we'll do very well together. May I ask if as yet you have an itinerary planned?" *No sense in letting this opportunity go unfulfilled.*

"Sir, yes, we have the beginnings of a list which, I'm told when finalized, will be sent up to you soonest. Sir," he said. "I do know that they include some trials, a trip to our Militia Academy, one more to our Combat Training bases, and I think one more over to our planet space center too. That might be a bit of a surprise, in that I'm not sure that the RIM even knows we have one. Course, without FTL, as you can probably tell, Captain, it's not what I'm sure you would call a tech marvel in any way, shape, or form, Sir," he said.

His voice, Tanner thought, was only a bit apologetic; strains of Enkian pride could still be heard. The alien seemed to stop for a moment and then started up again.

"Sir, tomorrow, I would like to take you to a juror trial over in the Dance Muse pyramid, for you to see a trial that we know will cause problems—the actual verdict we know about up front as the jurors always announce same to the Militia beforehand. Confidential, of course, but it does allow us to be forewarned—and forearmed too. It would be a whole day trip for us if that's ... if that's allowed for you to be away that long, Sir?"

Tanner thought about that for all of a nanosecond and then nodded slowly.

This will work out perfectly, he thought. *Watching what happens in a closed society like the Enki one, when there will be an unpopular decision could tell me much.*

"I will be ready when you tell me to—I'll take a shuttle down to the Words Muse pyramid we are using as home base, and I will be on time."

The stonecraw said, "Roger, Sir, see you tomorrow then," and he signed off.

"Interesting," Tanner said to himself, "this was very interesting." The ambassador had obviously worked hard on this, but this personal contact was also worthy of more study. *Must speak to Bram later on this.* He went back to his console and the damn reports all captains were required to fill out and sign.

#####

At the edge of the large open sand space in front of the Words Muse pyramid, Stonecraw Qew was waiting at the door of the bus idling in front of Tanner and Bram as they stepped out of their shuttle. It was already hot even though sunup had only happened about an hour ago; the two were drenched in sweat as they walked across the sand and quickly hustled up and into the air-conditioned bus.

"Good timing, and let's go" Stonecraw Qew said and nodded to the driver who wore the double stripes of a corporal.

The bus lurched as it gained purchase in the sands and then rolled off toward the far sand ridge against the horizon.

"Stonecraw, may I ask about the ranks in the Enkian Resources forces?" Bram said and then sat back in the almost comfortable bus seating.

Tanner thought about it and realized that knowing who and what the ranks were would be a good thing to have, as they'd be meeting more of same throughout the day.

"We—like many other military or paramilitary forces—have the standard type of ranks. At the lower end are the enlisted men—though we are all enlistees, come to think of it—and those ranks run private, corporal, sergeant, and then master sergeant. Our NCO ranks run same as what you'd find on UrPoPo, for example, and I'm sure that they are likely same in the various RIM forces too. Warrant officer, chief warrant officers, and warrant specialists too. Our officers are slightly different, we know, with lieutenants, stonecraws, captains, majors, colonels, and finally the topmost rank, our condas—you call them generals, I believe," he said, and Tanner nodded.

"Your ranks are very similar. Why is that, and maybe more importantly, how is that possible?" he asked, and he also sent out a mental note to Bram to see if the Enkian was telling the truth or not.

Stonecraw Qew nodded back to him. "It's pretty easy to see how that happened, Captain. We have been monitoring all the communications that one can gather from UrPoPo over the past few thousand years. We, unlike them, have not taken the tack that we should upgrade our technology year after year. So UrPoPo has FTL and we do not. But we do have Resources that track what UrPoPo does in all things. We have been watching them for hundreds of generations, and a part of that watching included their military forces too. From what little we know about the RIM Confederacy, we know that UrPoPo is considered a very small, inconsequential planet. Yet we watch them, as they are so close to us, and we have learned much—even that the language we now speak to the RIM group was learned from our monitoring them. And so our copying of many of the same military ranks was also learned. We did change a few things, though, as you can tell, to reflect what our Enkian forefathers must have decided needed doing."

He smiled and the three of them looked out of the side windows of the bus, and sand dune after sand dune went by.

After an hour of this brown vista, Tanner caught himself twice as he almost nodded off. "At least," he said to himself, "the bus has AC else this would be a sweaty ride." The sun beat down still as they rose on the crest of a dune, and ahead laid their destination or at least Tanner hoped so.

"That's the Dance Muse pyramid, yes, and we've made good time," Stonecraw Qew said as the bus pulled up at an access ramp.

The three of them hustled out of the bus and quickly across the baking hot sands to the stairs down into the tunnels below. Like all access points to pyramids, it grew nice and cool as they went down and down and then doubled back to take the long tunnel over to the basement area of the Dance Muse pyramid. At the bottom of the stairs to go up, a Resources colonel met them. About twenty feet away, seated on the floor, were at least fifty more Resources forces in full gear.

Each, Tanner could see, wore desert sand

camouflage fatigues and had sidearms and full side-
packs of other gear.

"Sir," Stonecraw Qew said to his colonel, "we just
arrived, and I'm wondering if we should go straight
up?"

He did not snap to attention. *Different strokes for
different folks*, Tanner thought, *is what made the galaxy
rotate.*

The colonel looked at first Bram, then Tanner,
and finally to his stonecraw and nodded. "Jurors are
just filing in upstairs, and the case results will be
stated in just a few minutes, so yes, get right up
there. Stay on the far side too, away from the stairs
and the heavy Performance Muse seating on the
south side too. If there's any issues, it'll occur there,"
he said, and his voice was matter-of-fact, but Tanner
could hear he was a bit worried.

As they climbed the stairs quickly, Stonecraw
Qew gave them a quick backstory on the case.
Performance Muse had brought a suit against
Dance Muse on the strength of a new play they had
been showcasing for over a month. Performance
said they had proof that Dance had taken materials
—dances, music, songs, words—the base items that
Performance had licensed for the show from other
muses—and stolen it for themselves.

"Yes," Qew said, "there was a short Dance
presentation that they were using as a part of the

whole show as a promotional item only. They were not charging any kind of price for this presentation, they showed it all over and often, and yes, it was in their opinion the best dance number in the show. Performance, however, made the claim that this presentation 'gutted' their own much larger show by taking the one show-stopping dance number and offering it up for free."

Tanner nodded and thought that under that kind of pressure, yes, the revenues for the overall show itself might suffer. *Wonder how that will play out,* he thought and realized he'd soon know.

As they mounted the final bank of stairs, Tanner was surprised to see the space that could have held thousands held fewer than five hundred. He followed Qew as he walked around the large open rotunda space, and they took seats against the far wall of bleachers, in the very front row. Across from them, the first few rows of seating were all filled solidly with what Qew said were Performance Muse citizens. To Tanner, they seemed fairly low key and didn't fidget as they awaited the case verdict. To their left sat mostly Dance Muse citizens, and they, by comparison, were anything but calm. Some carried signs that Tanner couldn't read as they were written in the Enkian language. Others were clacking their beaks, the clicks loudly echoing well above them into the eaves of the pyramid surrounding them.

The head juror, Iavoesi Qax, rose, and with a ripple of the green and gold feathered crest on his head, the crowd quieted quickly.

Out of the corner of his eye, Tanner could see the colonel of the Resources squad now standing on the stairs, near the top, but not very visible in the rotunda.

Watching, I'd say and yet, I wonder what the big deal is here. So one muse loses, so what? The matter certainly can't be that serious an issue—revenues, yes, are important, but it was still not that important. At least to me, Tanner thought.

"Enkians, the jurors have been considering this Claim by the Performance Muse and Dance Muse, and we have come to a decision, one that was a unanimous decision by the jurors." As usual, the crowd was silent and waited with bated breath.

Qax looked first at the Performance Muse citizens on one set of bleachers and then at the Dance Muse citizens on the other side. He then looked at the five leaders of the Performance Muse who sat in front of him, leaned their way on the stage on the dais, and cawed loudly, "Performance, Performance, Performance" as the winning side of the case.

Most cases ended quietly, but not this one, and even Tanner, who'd never even seen one before, was surprised at the sudden vigor of the whole slew of Dance Muse citizens who rose up and began to chant something in Enkian. They said the same phrase, "Snakth no finister," over and over.

Tanner looked at the colonel who was holding his squad still behind him and lower on the stairs.

"That is Enkian, Captain, and it means—um, that the verdict is bad—er, false, maybe. It is usually made by citizens who lose a case verdict—oh, oh—"

The Dance Muse citizens were now all moving toward the stage, carrying those placards and chanting the same refrain repeatedly. From somewhere in the back of the group of a few hundred upset citizens, someone threw a bottle of water at the stage, and it broke open on one of the tables on the stage drenching some of the jurors. That got a big hurrah from the Dance Muse citizens, who now were moving even more quickly toward the stage.

There were shouts from the Resources squad as they now poured into the large open rotunda. The colonel led one group to try to intercept the Dance Muse contingent, while others were running to the stage to try to get the jurors off safely, Tanner thought.

As he turned to his right a bit, he could see the quickest of the Performance Muse citizens grabbing some of the Dance Muse citizens and punches were thrown. Melees broke out as the two groups met, and the squad of Resources was too late to stop that.

Grabbing Bram, he said, "jurors!" As they had a closer vantage point, he ran to the stage. Tanner went up the stairs quickly as some Dance Muse followers reached the stage from the other side. He moved quickly to the center of the stage, grabbed Qax's arm, and moved the head juror behind him as Bram grabbed another juror. They backed up and that moved the jurors behind them to the edge of the stage. When the first rounds were heard, Tanner wished for his Colt, but he was unarmed.

Stonecraw Qew fired again and then one more time—three rounds into the air that went up a long way, and the ricochets could be heard way above their heads inside the stone pyramid.

Everyone froze, except for the Resources squad, who now were all over the stage and taking charge. Tanner was more than happy to give up his juror to someone in desert camouflage. The Performance Muse and Dance Muse citizens out on the rotunda floor slowly split apart, and the fighting was over. Both sides separated and moved to one side. The Performance citizens' feathered crests were all puffy with their purple and orange colors. Dance citizens, having lost first the verdict and then just a moment ago, this revolt in the rotunda, had their own crests, gray on brown, not at all puffed up and out. Instead, they all looked frustrated and beaten.

The colonel stood at the center of the stage and addressed all the occupants in the rotunda, his voice loud and strident. "You Dance citizens, clear this space immediately. You will leave here in the next five minutes or we will arrest you and take you in for failing to obey a Resources commander. You have five minutes. Performance citizens, please go about your business now. We will be here in the rotunda monitoring your compliance. That is all," he said, and the whole squad of his forces spread out to circle the stage and face outward as the citizens began to disperse.

After he finished, he quickly moved off the stage and came over to stand directly in front of Tanner. "Captain, I watched as you took the initiative and quickly put yourself between the head juror and the crowds as they mounted the stage. My commendations will be made to my superiors—but on behalf of the Enkian justice system, thank you, Sir," he said as both hands snapped to his chest in the traditional Enkian salute.

Standing still quite close, the head juror also came over, and as his feathered crest rippled, he too nodded to Tanner and thanked him profusely.

Tanner came to attention and replied with his

own Navy salute, and they smiled at each other.
The colonel and head juror moved off toward the
jurors who were all milling about just a few feet
away.

The three of them turned to watch the crowds
disperse the rotunda area.

Tanner watched and noted that even as the Dance
citizens were leaving, they were grumbling to each
other as they went down the stairs to the tunnels
back to the access ramp across the sands. Bram
watched too and then turned to his captain.

"Did you note that the Dance Muse group was
still upset? Don't think that a few warning shots
really did much to quell their anger either. Least as
far as I can tell," Bram said which received a nod
from Stonecraw Qew.

"Exactly as I see it," he said, and his feathers
rippled slightly. "The Dance citizens were upset—
and to my mind rightfully so. I believe that they
were given a bad verdict, but then that is the usual
thing about any kind of a verdict lately," he said as
he shook his head.

Now that was interesting, Tanner thought. "Tell me
more—what do you mean by that, exactly,
Stonecraw?"

The soldier moved closer to them as they now too
were going down the stairs to the tunnel below.
"Only that the current rumors are all about the head

juror—Iavoesi Qax—and how his last set of
verdicts has been generally seen as—well,
misguided is the word that is being used. Me? I'd
perhaps use a different word—biased comes to
mind," he said.

As they settled on the bus and prepared for the
long trip back to the Words Muse pyramid and the
Atlas shuttle, they kept Stonecraw Qew talking and
learned much about the usual juror verdicts and
that lately there had been a change.

#####

As the shuttle flew north, Tanner and Bram along
with Stonecraw Qew sat and looked out of the
windows at the changing landscape below. For
more than half an hour, the sands that were
normally below the shuttle were changing. Instead
of the huge flat plains with few dunes and ridges,
rippling dunes hundreds of feet high in some cases
were now below them. It had been minute after
minute of the same brown sand-colored
background, but when you took the time to stare at
the formations and sculpture of the sand itself, it
was impressive. Nobody could see any water, but
occasionally there was a copse of some kind of local
trees with sparse grasses and even some kind of low
shrub. Tanner thought these might be called oases,
but he really didn't know for sure. There hadn't

been more than a handful as they continued to fly north at about a thousand feet up. No water in any sizable amount meant, as far as he knew, no life could exist. That was pretty much a given, but then again, he'd seen some pretty strange things on planets all over the RIM and inward too. Still the dunes were magnificent, rolling and yet sculpted with sharp edges too. And on they still flew, and he could see on the horizon a different color—not so brown but sort of a brownish-green coloration. He watched as the new colored horizon slowly came closer, and then he noticed the dunes had changed. Instead of being free-formed, running in whatever direction or shape that they had so far, now they tended to run diagonally, as if they were sculpted by winds that blew from northwest to southeast.

"Absolutely correct," Qew said, "due to the prevailing winds here in the temperate zones. It's here that those winds with no moisture left in them still have enough power to shape the dunes. This area runs almost a thousand miles thick, encircling the globe both above and below our own living zone around the Enkian equator," he added.

Below, there were small sand devils that were whipping up the sides of the dunes. Qew had informed them that the small dust storms occurred often.

In less than an hour, the shuttle still climbed

north by northwest, and the dunes grew bigger, as
did the sand devils too, and eventually on the
horizon, the color changed from sand brown to a
dark green shade.

"We're coming up to the edge of the sand
country," Qew said, and he pointed out a side
viewport at what lay ahead.

Those sand dunes were now smaller and smaller,
and yes, eventually they petered out onto flat bare
rock and dirt and the start of some vegetation. As
the shuttle moved on northward, the vegetation
became greener and the rock and dirt less
noticeable until there was nothing but fields of what
looked like grass with only marginal patches of
sand. The climate was changing below them, and
Qew spoke up on that too.

"Enki is hot—you have learned that already. But
due to the oddly flattened spherical shape of the
planet, here above the fiftieth parallel, the ground
falls away much quicker. Hence, the lack of the
huge heated climate, and as a result, it's where Enki
has all of its agriculture—our farms as you call
them," he said, and sure enough in a few minutes
more, Tanner looked down and saw big agriculture
all over the horizon.

The Enki farms were automated with vast
irrigation systems and water sprinklers too, and
while they were too high to identify what crops lay

below, the fields were full of heavy rows of foliage that stretched on for as far as they could see.

Up ahead, there was what looked like a small city — or a big town perhaps. Rows of streets were aligned with the river that ran through the town's center, and if pushed, Tanner thought he'd have to estimate there'd be five to ten thousand inhabitants there. As it was daytime, there was no way to tell what kind of lighting they used or how they powered their towns. In fact, he suddenly realized, he had no idea how the muse pyramids were powered either and made a PDA note to check on that when they returned.

As the shuttle pilot, Lieutenant Jenkins, yawed the shuttle to respond to an incoming base message, Tanner saw a Militia base below them.

"Sir," Jenkins said, "we have been granted landing privileges, and we'll touch down in a few moments."

The shuttle turned once more to port and slowly began to sink down toward the surface. As the shuttle moved down, Tanner noted that a small personnel carrier was coming out toward them and thought this would be their landing greeting party. A few minutes later when the shuttle doors opened up, a small Enkian group greeted him.

What appeared to be a leader in that group stepped forward, and in Enkian, he yelled out what sounded like orders. *Whatever this guy just said was certainly not "welcome." I know that much!*

Qew, however, got in Tanner's way and led them out while barking orders in Enkian to the group. Tanner noted there was at least one senior officer who seemed to resent Qew taking over, but all of the greeting group moved back and stood off to one side.

Qew smiled at the humans and nodded over to the group. "It appears that while we were expected, someone here had assumed that we were going to be entering the base—not as visitors but as some kind of a task force that was due today to do some kind of an audit. That's not us and while they weren't happy to learn that, that's their problem and not ours," he finished off.

Gesturing for Tanner and Bram to follow him, he turned and marched off around the personnel carrier, and they all aimed at the far set of buildings to the east away from the landing area.

"There is grass on a desert planet," Bram commented and smiled.

Tanner hadn't spent much time so far on this trip thinking about the planet itself and how it was able to support itself, but that too was an area he should PDA himself on as well.

As they walked, Qew pointed out some of the training sessions that were going on around them.

"Close order drill for that squad," he said as he pointed over to the west side of the field.

There, a group of fifty Militia members was being put through their paces by a drill sergeant, Tanner thought. No matter what military for what race, that kind of task required a drill sergeant who could rack up days and weeks of intensive training for the recruits—and there was no difference here on Enki. While he couldn't understand the sergeant's comments, he knew what the alien was saying nonetheless. Recruits were falling all over themselves trying to keep up. The drill sergeant was having none of that, and he barked constantly at them to get more focus, more involvement, and more output.

As they moved farther away, the taunting and complaining of the sergeant faded away and reinforced for Tanner that military training was of supreme importance no matter where it happened.

At the building just ahead, Qew turned to speak to them, and they all stopped short of entering.

"Small point here, Captain. That as a visitor group, we will need to follow base rules, and that means that we will have to accept what they've arranged for us inspection-wise and anything else that they've worked on for us to see. Hope that this is acceptable, Captain?" he said and Tanner could tell he was a bit concerned too.

"Not a problem, Stonecraw — we are yours for the day," he answered, and he and Bram nodded to the alien.

Nodding, he moved a few steps, opened up the door, and ushered them inside.

Just like any other base offices, Tanner thought as he looked around. *Waiting room with chairs, desk with an aide or two, and more offices down a hallway.*

They took seats while Qew went up to the aide and appeared to ask a question. Qew returned a moment later to speak to Tanner and Bram.

"Conda Qip will be a few minutes, but we're going to have a minute or two with him. Aide says that they've planned out most of our day — but that we do have some free time later right after the lunch break, it appears. If we can get it crammed in, I'd like to take you over to the big new obstacle course — something that I'm especially proud of in fact," he said.

Moments later, the conda's aide said something to Qew in Enkian, and he rose and led the way into the inner office.

It was an office, at least that's what they expected to see, yet Tanner couldn't help but feel that this wasn't meant for visitors to see — to experience.

Inside at a desk in the far corner, the conda sat — an Enkian Militia member who was bigger than most. A tall, tall feathered crest in the black and lavender colors was the first thing you saw. The feathers were taller than any that Tanner had ever seen before. But it was the beak on the alien's face that was so different, as at some point, this had been injured, and there was a large scar of some kind that went obliquely across the whole shell of his beak. It was stained black, and Tanner had no idea why it was like that, but overall, it gave this conda a look that said "I do not fool around" and that was imposing. But the rest of the office was still odder.

On his left, one wall held photos, dozens of photos, of what looked like recruit training exercises, more of groups of recruits at their graduation perhaps, and still more of some kind of a major battle. The photo was too small for Tanner to see who was fighting and why they were fighting, but Tanner knew combat photos, and that's what these were.

Combat against who? Enki was alone—they had only UrPoPo as close neighbors and there was no war there. Tanner made a mental note to check on that as he looked over to his right side at the remaining wall of the office.

Against one wall was some kind of Enkian sculptures—perhaps they were trophies, Tanner thought, as he noted the dozen that sat on a long counter. Each was jet black with lavender highlights as per the Militia color palette. Yet each was of a dead, or perhaps only dying, Enkian lying at the feet of a standing Militia forces soldier. Each of the dead or dying Enkians had the feathered crest of a muse—the Words Muse red and white on one, and the Fine Arts Muse blue and red on another. The victory of the Militia over the muses was how Tanner read these, and he looked back at the conda sitting in front of them with more interest.

Speaking Enkian, Qew made a statement or two after coming to attention with an Enkian salute. That was ignored by the conda, who simply sat, listened, and then nodded. Nothing was ever said so they might understand, Tanner realized. That was a small thing, yet in the world of intel, it was a big thing for future considerations. *Big indeed ...*

As the two Enkians finished their quick chat, the conda rose, smiled—at least Tanner interpreted it as a smile——and in pretty good English wished them a great visit. Then without any further ado, he sat back down and they were dismissed. *Like all command officers, next is what is now.* Tanner smiled and nodded his thanks.

Outside, the aide handed Qew a short visitor itinerary, and he nodded to her as they left the command offices and went back outside to the field.

Qew pointed over to a long, low single-floor building off to the left and began walking toward it.

"First stop today will be combat training, if that's

okay?" he asked, but Tanner thought that no matter what he said, they were going to follow the itinerary as closely as was possible. As they walked along, Qew expounded on the Militia training regimen.

"We get the younglings at twelve years of age, and yes, they are all pre-sorted for us," he said.

Bram said, "Pre-sorted, Qew?"

"Sorry, yes—as you know, younglings are raised up until the age of twelve in our society. At that time, they are tested for the five muses—should they show promise for any of them, they are then sorted into those streams. Some, however, are better suited for military training—our Militia. Others for management of Enkian resources so they go that way. No matter, but by the age of twelve, we have our annual recruits. Here at this base, as well as at any of the more than fifty bases worldwide, they are trained to be Militia soldiers. Full and complete training. And it's the combat basics that you'll be seeing in just a few minutes ..."

Bram spoke up quicker than Tanner. "Younglings come from where exactly, Qew?" His voice was questioning but it was easy to tell that this was a new term for him.

Qew rippled his crest. "Did no one explain about Enkian younglings to you as yet?" he asked, his voice a bit exasperated.

Tanner and Bram shook their heads negatively.

"Okay, here's what you need to know. Once a year, our Enkian females enter a short reproductive season that lasts just a few days. If she is lucky enough to mate with an Enkian male, then about fifty days later, she bears an egg. These eggs are collected, of course, by our Resources teams and stored away in incubators 'til they hatch into our younglings. Resources looks after them 'til they reach the age of twelve when they are then sorted as to their futures. You didn't know any of that?" he asked, his voice assuming this was true.

Tanner stopped in his tracks. "If what you say is true, then once the egg is taken to Resources, there is no—um—no family tie between the mother and the youngling, correct?" he said.

"Why would there need to be? It's Resources that is in charge of raising our younglings, not the mothers," Qew said, and he looked a bit exasperated once again.

Tanner nodded. *This might explain much,* he thought and again made a note to himself that he would need to pass this along to the ambassador et al.

Bram had been looking into the stonecraw's mind and here. He thought the stonecraw might be a good candidate for an input test.

Stonecraw Qew had the same rows and huge

columns of filing cabinets like all the Enkians. He
was about thirty years of age, male, and in the
military. Bram mentally ticked off those
checkboxes, as he'd have to remember them too. So
far, Bram had been watching Stonecraw Qew
carefully, trying to gauge his every sentence for
where it came from in the filing cabinet rows and
what was behind it. He could also look ahead at
least a few minutes too for the Enkian—for
instance, in a few minutes he might speak up on a
young recruit who would almost injure another.

He stood just to the stonecraw's left, and he
gazed into the Enkians mind. Ahead just a moment
was the path they would take inside this new
building, and he could see the real path was off to
the left-hand side corridor. Bram concentrated on
the opposite. He pushed the new path of going to
the right instead of the left into that filing cabinet
and imagined that the small card labeled with "path
to the gym" was on the drawer, and he dropped out
of the Enkian's mind.

As they entered the low building ahead, Qew
moved them into the foyer, hesitated, and then
turned to the right. The three of them moved
quickly along a side hallway to a larger corridor
that led back to administrative offices—row and
row of them—ahead.

They continued to walk and received a few stares

from other Enkians in Militia camouflage clothing, but no one stopped them. At the end of the long, long hallway, they turned to their left, went all the way across the back of the building, turned once more to their left, and strode along the long hallway.

About halfway down that corridor, they turned to their left into a big gym that they could hear was full of some kind of training session.

As they entered the room, Qew held out an arm to stop them short of the actual floor and nodded for them to follow him around the side wall to a set of raised bleachers to go and sit down.

Bram nodded to himself and tested the input test too.

"Stonecraw, wasn't there a shorter way to the gym?" Bram thought a direct challenge might be the way.

Stonecraw Qew nodded and held up his hands, palms up.

"Sure is but I just thought that you'd all appreciate the walk around the building seeing us Militia types all working and such," he said.

Bram could see there was no truth to that as the Enkian's mind knew this was a fib although one of no real merit or worth.

Input test administered, and yes, I can affect an Enkians mind enough to gain a small amount of control.

He knew that reporting that would get the Master to tell him to escalate the value of the test, eventually challenging the Enkians with major choices of morality or politics or the like.

EYES ONLY needed, Bram thought.

As they made their way to some raised seating, the recruits below them, numbering over one hundred, finished up their calisthenics and were guided by sergeants out on the floor into two lines each facing another. One of the sergeants addressed them all in Enkian for a few moments, and they paired off with a fellow recruit in the facing lineup. At the sergeant's command that was barked out, one whole row went on the attack, while their counterpart in the facing row went on the defensive. Sergeants moved among the rows pointing out mistakes and barking at their recruits as those mistakes happened.

Tanner paid specific attention to the pair closest to them to see what they were practicing.

One recruit was on the attack, and he shook his hands, his feathered crest rippling like water on a rapids. He took a step forward, then sideways, and then forward again. His counterpart retreated too in the same kind of stepped formation.

Suddenly the attacking recruit stepped over one leg with the other, planted it with a slap, and then whirled in a half-circle.

The newly planted foot rotated as the now free leg circled like a whip, and his spur on the rear of that foot lashed out at the defending recruit.

That recruit was not quick enough, so the spur caught him across one thigh and ripped a gash right through his camouflage leggings.

Without some kind of armor below those leggings, the recruit would have been badly slashed, but all that Tanner could hear was the scrape of the spur along the under-armor accompanied by a huge screech.

The two recruits nodded to each other, and then the roles were reversed.

"Typical attack move," Stonecraw Qew said, "yet very well done—that recruit should be watched carefully."

Bram noted the comment that had been made was the one he had seen in the stonecraw's mind earlier. That meant he could see what an Enkian intended to say at least a few minutes before the Enkian said it.

Impressive tactical move, Tanner thought, as he watched dozens and dozens of the recruits do the same exact step-over leg whip. Some spurs hit their targets. Others missed the target or were blocked.

Without a weapon, he thought, *this was a good move by an Enkian, and I'll have to remember this for future safety ...*

#####

The Master Adept was the last one to join the rest of the Executive Committee members for the monthly meeting. *If one could tell,* the Baroness thought, *the woman was not her usual calm self. Wonder what is upsetting her,* but then she realized she would probably soon know.

"Let's come to order, shall we?" Chairman Gramsci said, and he referred to the printed Agenda that lay in front of him, as he began to read.

Moments later, he stopped and looked at the sealed envelope beside his Agenda and said, "This is unusual," as he picked up the envelope and opened it to read the report it contained.

The rest of the Committee sat and waited. The Baroness wondered why he'd gotten the only copy of the report. The Master Adept of Eons looked instead at the table in front of her and said not a word. The Duke d'Avigdor toyed with a stylus on his tablet and he too said nothing. The Caliph just stared at the chairman at an impasse. The doge of Conclusion did the same, and only the admiral of the RIM Navy said anything at all.

"Unusual, but necessary, as this will undoubtedly be seen, Chairman. This is my doing—we will await your reading and understanding of the report," he finished off and sat back.

The three-page report took the chairman almost five whole minutes to read and to digest.

He put it down and nodded. "Admiral, thank you for your report—although I believe this may pose more problems for the RIM than opportunities. At least at first glance ..."

The Baroness exploded. "What in all things that are holy is this all about?" she sputtered and slapped her hand down hard onto the round table they all were seated at.

The chairman nodded and he slid the report over to her as he began to speak.

"The admiral—well, I guess it was the RIM Navy itself, took ownership of that probe from Enki. You might remember that they sent us an acknowledgment of our initial invite to begin talks to join the RIM Confederacy more than seventy years ago. Well, this probe was sent to the Navy labs for testing. Plain Jane type of AI, keyed to mount its top speed of about one-half light speed per year, which is why it took so long for it to get here. But that is not the sum of the report—what is important are the results of the hull testing," he said, and he had everyone's attention.

As he continued, the Baroness put down the report and paid attention too, to get his take on the subject.

"Simply put, the metal used to build the probe is an unknown metal made from an ore that we have no similar element on our charts. This is a brand new metal, and so it was subjected to a whole host of tests," he said, and all of the heads of state at the table leaned in.

"As expected, the projectile testing—where various size caliber weapons are shot at the metal—showed nothing special at all. Piercings occurred as expected and were tracked, and the analytics are available for anyone here to see. But it was the Ray testing that was the unusual item—the metal appears to be invulnerable to any kind of our ray weapons," he said quietly.

The table exploded.

"Exactly what does that mean—" the doge started.

"How reliable are these tests—" the Caliph said.

"Not the energy pulse weapons—they destroy everything—" the duke began.

"Silence!" the Master Adept said, and this was so unusual that all became instantly silent.

The chairman nodded to her, offering her the chance to have the floor and to speak.

"I saw this, of course, and must ask you all to consider something both pro and con on this matter —a metal that if we can gain its ownership—we can help keep our own ships safer. Yes, I know that this

is the major thought in each of your minds. And I
also see the wheels turning about how to turn this
into a revenue stream for each of your realms. I get
that. I understand that. But what each of you does
not know is that this metal is found only on Enki. It
belongs to them—and at this point, we do not even
know if they will join the RIM Confederacy. You
are now all hoping so—but consider this too. That
even should they join, once they learn that this
metal is a major product that they will control and
own—and yes, I see that all of you are thinking the
same thing. You will take it if you cannot get it any
other way ..."

She shook her finger at them all before
continuing.

"And it is that thought of war here on the RIM
that I speak against today. War cannot come to the
RIM —ever," she said, and that last sentence hung
there for all to hear again in their ears.

She sat back. She had spoken. The Baroness now
realized what had set the Master Adept off and
why she was so upset.

Still, the ability to shield a ship from lasers and
energy pulse weapons or plasma cannons was a
thing to be wished for and yes, well worth the
effort. Still, short of a war, the only other thing that
might work would be diplomatic negotiations of the
highest order.

The chairman thanked the Master for her opinions, and they went around the table for each member of the Executive Committee to have their opinions known and heard.

The doge of Conclusion, while twirling the white hair on the back of one hand with the other, offered that yes, they would need to somehow gain access to the ores to make it themselves ... but yes, he'd support a diplomatic slow course to gain that access.

The Caliph, however, was a bit more blunt. He wanted only to get the metal for his ships, he said. He'd pay for it or take it. He didn't care much about the Enkians at all. The Master flinched during his short statement, and the Baroness could tell she could see more than they had all heard.

For her own part, the Baroness said that yes, they would like the metal too for their own ships—and she would simply follow the lead of the rest of the Committee too. *She knew there would be an answer today on this. It was important,* she thought, *that the consensus be the acquiring of the metal no matter how that was accomplished.*

Duke d'Avigdor mirrored her own comments and said he'd also follow the Committee consensus, and he hoped that the answers would come via diplomacy rather than by force.

Lastly, the chairman spoke, and he too said he'd

support diplomacy as the first attempt at acquiring the metals for the use of same here on the RIM. And he called for a vote—and the diplomatic approach was the result of their consensus.

Instructing the admiral on what that would entail took a few hours more as they argued about the offer their ambassador currently carried and how that offer could be sweetened without giving away their knowledge about the metal. That too took some work, but eventually they crafted a sweetened offer and even a "cherry on top" that the admiral posed, which had them all enthused too.

The admiral took on the job of sending off the new instructions to the ambassador via an EYES ONLY later that day.

As she left the room, the Baroness nodded to the Master Adept and noted that her gaze was met and fully returned.

She liked it when they seemed to be on the same page as they said. This new opportunity might bode well for both their realms.

CHAPTER FOUR

On the *Atlas*, one of the best things that Tanner had learned was that the cooks on-board were the best he'd ever had the pleasure of serving with in any man's navy. Sure, he'd enjoyed the food on the *Kerry* and the *Marwick* when he was in the RIM Confederacy Navy, but the Barony Navy was a full level up when it came to both menu and the wide variety of ethnic cooking styles from different planets.

Tanner's favorite was the nights when the cooks took on what they called Asian cooking, and that included his favorite Thai items like Pad Thai and Tom Yam Goong or Som Tam with its spicy papaya spicing, which made him grin from ear to ear. Like most almost forty-year-old people, Tanner realized worrying about his uniform pants getting a bit tight was a new thing to worry about. Yet on Asian nights, he said the hell with it and chowed down on all the various items that came out of the kitchen—and he usually told the stewards to bring more too. He was not too proud of it, but he tried to always ride herd on his waistline on all other nights, but never on Asian night.

And tonight, he'd sent a note to the cooking staff with a special request to please provide their best Asian menu for dinner as he was entertaining some visitors from Enki. He'd heard back that the cooks were planning a real feast this evening including, he'd heard, some items they had never added to the banquet menu before. He had smiled with delight and had checked a few times with the bridge stewards that yes, all was well down in the dining room and the dining event would be perfect.

He surely hoped so, as tonight he was hosting the RIM ambassador, the five leaders of the Words Muse, and a selected smaller group too—including, he had insisted, on his newfound friend, Stonecraw Qew and a couple more members of the Resources team too. He had asked Qew if Conda Qip, whom they had just met at the Resources training facility a day ago or so, could make it. That wouldn't be possible, Qew had confirmed, but he thanked the RIM group very much for the invite.

Nice to see, at least on the surface of things if he

could believe what he'd been told, that the Enkians were also well mannered enough to know that one should always send thanks along with regrets. *Good to know*, Tanner thought, and *hopefully one more sign that the RIM and Enki might find a way to work out their differences.*

He smiled at Lieutenant Irving and waved her over to join him at his captain's station on the bridge.

"Lieutenant, just wanted to know if you've heard from Nathan—I mean, Research Team Leader Ward—as yet from Ghayth? Is he enjoying the setting up of the new labs? Where did they put him too?" he asked.

Lieutenant Irving was engaged to Ward, and while she was his best Ansible officer on the *Atlas*, her fellow was all the way across the RIM more than ninety lights away, where he was the new research Science officer there. His job had come from the Lady St. August after the attempt to steal the vaccine over on the Barony Hospital Ship and how he'd been manipulated by the Caliphate. It was part penance for his succumbing to the threats of the Caliph, but more than that, it was a fresh start, and both he and Lieutenant Irving had been overjoyed that Lady St. August had seen fit to give them that chance.

"Sir, he's loving it. We Ansible daily and while

Ghayth is pretty much a dreary place, he is in love with the pioneering aspect of the planet. No sentients have been found yet, but they've discovered a host of new flora and fauna. He's already talking about expanding his team, trying to get a new and bigger budget—all the items any team leader deals with, Sir. My thanks once again to both you and Lady St. August for this," she said, and she ducked her gaze down to the floor as she quickly wiped away a tear.

He reached out, squeezed her arm, and nodded. He said nothing, but he squeezed her arm a couple more times.

"Sir, while I know that I can't mention anything about our mission to him, can I tell him where we are—say just the UrPoPo system? Him not knowing seems like a big thing, and he's always asking me ..." She looked up at him.

He nodded. "Yes, I think the UrPoPo system is broad enough, and that'd be fine," he said, and she grinned at him as she snapped a quick salute and went back to her Ansible station toward the front of the bridge.

Tanner went back to his console as there were now more than a dozen flashing icons. Click one. Read the issue. Make a decision. Communicate back to the sender. Send. Time and time again, he did just that, and as the number went down every few minutes, it seemed to jump back up as well.

A captain's job was more administrative than he'd ever wanted, but there were good times too.

More than three hours later, he looked at his reflection in the mirror in his quarters to double-check his appearance.

Gray hair at his temples blended into his coal black hair, which looked a bit mature and distinguished he thought. His dress blues, with the campaign ribbons on the left breast, looked as dressy as possible, and his boots were spotless and shiny. He checked his Colt too; since the Hospital Ship event a few months back, he'd visited the *Atlas* arsenal and had drawn his favorite model Colt. He wore it on his side now just about all the time. It wasn't the desert finish that he liked, but even true-blue, it was a serious projectile weapon, and he checked it was on safety and double-clasped in his holster at his side.

Looks fine. And it's Asian night. He smiled, spun on a heel, went out onto Deck Four, and turned to his left as he went down the long deck corridor to the dinner party that was to be held in a conference room. It was down a fair piece, and as he walked the deck corridor, Tanner could see ahead that the tall stainless steel food carts were being wheeled in and there were a lot of them. A line of cooks was entering the room as well, and then he could see a brace of EliteGuards too, stationed outside in the corridor. As he walked, he saw there were guests a few hundred feet away being ushered in this direction, so he sped up a little to get there ahead of them.

At the doorway, he glanced in—the room looked beautiful. A large square table would seat the many guests, and there was a huge buffet line off to one side. A small contingent of Enkian chefs stood behind the trays of warming Enkian food or what passed for their food—pellets maybe. While he knew that Enkians could easily digest human food, he also knew they needed at least some of their specialized Enkian food too every day. Each of the muses and also Militia and Resources had to eat the chemically treated specialized Enkian food every day to keep their colorations of feathers fed and intact. He'd learned that from Stonecraw Qew on the way home from their visit to the training center just a few days ago. Every young Enkian stayed at the training center until each Enkian was judged and sorted on their graduation day. And that happened here in this city in less than three weeks.

Coming over to say hello, Steward Jim Ashley bustled over and grinned at him.

"Sir, what a great dinner party this will be! Everything is as you've ordered, and the cooks have gone all out, Sir. There's some new dishes, and I understand that they even got the chance to use some local Enkian products too. Congratulations, Sir ... I'm sure it will be a wonderful evening! And oh yes, we have that new tea station too—know that you've found a winner, so I personally stocked it for you," he said and smiled at his captain.

The smells were about the best Tanner had ever experienced—he knew this would be a wonderful meal. A real bonding event, he hoped.

Back at the doorway, Tanner took up a station by the door and was joined by Bram, his Adept Officer, and moments later his XO, Kondo Lazaro, and the invited dinner guests walked up to the doorway. His XO had been given the duty to meet all the guests and to escort them to the dinner party room, and they were all here, and Tanner thought, *all looked pretty snazzy.*

The RIM ambassador was at the head of the lineup, and he was most graceful and pleasing in giving thanks to Tanner for the wonderful dinner— and that made him laugh loudly.

"There's a rule in the Diplomatic Corps, Captain Scott—that one should always thank the host before the meal. Sort of an insurance against bad food, I suspect—but I'm told by everyone that the *Atlas* has the finest cooks in the RIM! So thanks once again, Captain," he said as he nodded to Tanner and went into the room. Following him were others from the ambassador's group. Next, the five head Enkians of the Words Muse presented themselves one by one, and each thanked Tanner for his hospitality and offered that they too were looking forward to a wonderful dinner. Behind them came the extra Words Muse followers who always accompanied their leaders. And finally, Tanner smiled, Stonecraw Qew and two more Militia officers presented themselves.

"Stonecraw Qew, how nice that you could join us this evening," he said, and he held out his hand to shake the Enkians.

That seemed to catch Stonecraw Qew off-guard, but a moment later, he too held out his hand and allowed Tanner to shake it a few times.

"This is called 'shaking hands,' Qew," Tanner said, "and it's a sign of respect, indicating that the two people respect each other."

Qew nodded back and smiled, rippling his feathered crest.

Seems like he likes being called a person that I respect, Tanner thought.

Looking down the corridor, he saw no one else. *Odd,* he thought, and he caught his XO's eye inside the room and waved him over.

"The *Marwick* crew?" he said.

"Sir, sorry—thought you knew. Recalled back to Faraway—the trade wars with Leudi have erupted, and I hear there are some casualties too. They jumped more than an hour ago, so sudden that I'd guess Captain Templeton didn't have time to say goodbye. Most likely, he'll Ansible you soon. Oh, and that means that—at least according to the Barony orders—we are now the 'ship of record' too. I hear that the ambassador has already been moved into one of those big owners quarters way forward, and his staff are bringing over his effects, files, and all the diplomatic stuff to the *Atlas*. We win—least that's how it looks, Sir," he said, and Tanner could catch only the tiniest bit of sarcasm in Kondo's voice.

"Um, okay ... that's news, but sure. No RIM Navy vessel sent out to replace the *Marwick*, I take it?"

"Sir—not at this point far as I know. We will be advised though, we were told," Kondo said.

Tanner raised an eyebrow, and it was met with the same look back from Kondo.

Having just been along for the ride was one thing —but now, the *Atlas* was the ship the ambassador called home, and that meant the rules might change for them all, but that remained to be seen.

The EYES ONLY was quickly Ansibled for Bram, and he took his place at his desk in his

quarters and waited for the face of his Master
Adept to resolve on his monitor screen. Moments
later, her face appeared, and the first thing that
Bram thought was that being the Master of the
Issians who could read minds looked like it took its
toll.

She looks tired, he thought, *and that's about as nice
as I can put it.*

There were lines in her face that he'd not noticed
before; crow's feet they were called, and on her face,
they were deep. Below them, the two lines that
normally ran down the side of the end of the nose
to the chin area were also deeply carved and the
shadows were blackened. Her normally bright
brown eyes were fine though less bright perhaps,
but the whites were heavily saturated with those
red blood vessels that one sees on faces that are so
troubled. Wearing her usual browns, her jersey had
some stains on it, he thought, and she was seated in
a chair that seemed too big for her, and she often
squirmed un-self-consciously it appeared to him
too.

"Master, I wanted to speak to you soon as I had
some results for those input testing events. And I
can report that they were all successful," he said as
he smiled at her.

She didn't smile back but her hand seemed to
flutter at him to quicken his report.

"Master, I tested twice for three different Enkian subjects," he said as he began to rattle off the details about the three Enkians he had tested.

"One was a Militia officer, male, about thirty years old. From him I was able to change a course of action, change a choice of food at a banquet, and change an opinion of some art that he was considering buying. Lastly, I was also able to read ahead for him almost by ten minutes too—a sign I think that speaks well for us.

"Number two was a much older female, one of the five leaders of the Words Muse, and I found her to be exactly the same. I was able to change her opinion in an upcoming case in their courts and change her ability to decide on who to hire for a new assistant and even on what to wear. I was, however, unable to see much of her future—only as far ahead as a mere two minutes. Both, however, were accurate."

He then presented his final case.

"Finally an opportunity presented itself when I went to a small art class in the Fine Arts Muse pyramid, where I sat with more than a dozen younglings—those are Enkians of less than twelve years of age. Each was the same. Each I could change from what color to use next on their paintings to what sculpture tools to use on their works in progress. I was also able to see well ahead

for them—more than a half hour ahead in all cases
—and all proved valid," he said with a small degree
of pride.

The Master nodded. "You have done well—and
apparently you have been fairly successful, Bram.
My thanks, but now to the meat of the matter," she
said, and it might have been Bram's connection, but
her face seemed to droop even more.

"We—well, those of us with the long-term sight
ability—have seen war ahead. There is no doubt, it
appears. And while at this point we do not have a
timeline on it, the war does appear to be somehow
linked to Enki. Our best and brightest have all been
called home to Eons for our work on what to do
about this. And you, you will be our Issian on the
scene. We will watch, and if an opportunity to help,
to mold, to modify this threat comes from your
position on Enki—then we will contact you
immediately. Understood, Adept?"

He nodded to his Master and the screen faded to
black. .

It was time, Tanner thought, *to double-check his
recon. If asked, I know what to say—but double-checking
the RIM ambassador is an iffy thing to do.* He truly felt
it was iffy and he sighed. "Yet," he said to "I have to
know more and that requires my own talks with the

Fine Arts Muse leaders.

He smiled at the EliteGuard who had just stuck his head in the doorway.

"If my guests are here, they are welcome," he said, and moments later, three Enkians walked into the small conference room on Deck Five, just near the bridge.

Bram, the *Atlas* Adept officer, greeted them, seated them, and had the stewards offer up refreshments, which took only a few minutes.

And then they all stared at Tanner as Bram dropped into a chair beside him on the *Atlas* side of the table.

Feathered crests of blue and red topped the heads of Fine Arts Muse Enkians, and it struck him those were the same exact colors of the Barony crest. "Noted," he said to himself, and he smiled at the leader of the muse, Eecesoe Qig. He was about average in height with the same plumage as all Enkians, but one thing was different—his hands looked strong with knotted veins and very muscular too. *Wonder what he does that gets his hands and forearms so built up.* But judging by the way they were all looking at him, they were waiting for something.

So he gave it to them.

"The RIM ambassador has taken me into his confidence—I understand that if we use whatever influence we have to get you the head juror's position, then you'll guarantee that Enki will become a RIM Confederacy member. Have I stated that deal—in its entirety—correctly, Qig?" he said.

The three Enkians sat back and looked among themselves, and after a second or two, they switched to Enkian. The conversation appeared to grow somewhat heated. One of the Fine Arts Muse leaders was shaking a talon at Qig and seemed to be counseling one thing, and both Qig and the remaining Enkian were counter-arguing. Tanner had no idea about what—and he made a mental note that he would see about getting someone to learn Enkian so that he and anyone else from the RIM could learn surreptitiously.

As he waited, he glanced over at Bram and raised an eyebrow.

Bram nodded and held up a single finger—his code that he had something but would wait until they were alone.

A minute or two later, the feathered crest on top of Qig's head rippled loudly, and it stopped their heated discussion abruptly.

Qig turned back to Tanner, dipped his head slowly, and then raised his eyes to stare directly into Tanner's.

"Captain—you have caught us by surprise, in that we did not expect our confidential discussions with the RIM ambassador to be shared. That said, you have stated the case—the deal as you have called it—almost in its entirety. One thing, however, you have not mentioned."

Qig looked up at the ceiling for a moment, and Tanner wondered if it was for some kind of memory that he was accessing or if he might be asking his deity—if Enkians even had one.

"What we have found, Captain, is that the muse —our muse I refer to—Fine Arts forbids the kind of friendship and intermingling that many other worlds and societies revel in. We see all non-muse Enkians as outsiders—as our enemies—who lack in the responsibility and accountability to be beholden to our values. They are not to be trusted, and as we see it, we Fine Arts Muse citizens are always right."

Tanner thought on that for a moment as Qig took a brief second to gather more thoughts. *It's like he's talking about a cult or a religion rather than a group of aliens who can all paint well. This was a bit odd*, he thought, as Qig looked at him once more.

"As well, Captain, we have our own Fine Arts sacred books—like all the Enkian muses have their own—and our books remind our muse citizens about what our muse is all about. About how ours is the only muse that is silent—all of the others require one to listen to something—words or acting or music or dances. Ours is the only reflective muse where one turns inwards to see what is inside each of us as one gazes at a painting or a sculpture for example. All the others depend on audio input—ours, of course, as the superior muse is the only one that is silent. It allows us to reflect on our own feelings, our temperament, our superiority—all are found inside each of us and, as our sacred books relate, are a Fine Arts Muse citizen's privilege."

His tone was solemn and reverential, Tanner thought, *just like a religious leader, and that might be only a facet of this single muse. Or was it*

Qig looked down at his hands, each clasped together, holding on it appeared, but for what Tanner wondered.

We will soon know. He again sipped his tea as the Fine Arts Muse leader took a moment to couch his answer.

"Captain, the only part that you did not mention was the penalty that we would inflict should you not be successful," he said slowly.

"You mean, of course, what the Fine Arts Muse would do if you do not get the head juror position, correct?" Tanner asked.

"Yes, Captain—we would then file cases with the jurors to keep Enki out of the RIM Confederacy. While this sounds like a small thing, let me assure you that in the Enkian judicial system, filing just such a case then would put the issue—our joining the RIM Confederacy—on hold until the case is fully heard and deposed and decided. And, we also would file these cases one by one for all of our more than millions of Fine Arts Muse citizens. One by one. We do have some estimations that this would take over four hundred years, which would also, of course, put the rest of the judicial system on hold. Nothing else would be heard or decided. The turmoil, we think, would be astronomical—more than has ever happened before on Enki. And yes, we realize that this is an extreme penalty—but we have no choice. Enki cannot endure a slide to the right that would occur if the Words Muse leader, Uigoeri Qor, should be elected to the head juror position. We will do anything to prevent that move to ultra-conservatism. Anything—as you can tell," he said, and those hands were clenched so tightly that Tanner could see the veins were distended and pulsing rapidly.

He looked at Bram for a moment and then back to the Enkians across the table.

"Understood, Qig. We did not know about that, um, penalty as you call it. But it is noted, and I perhaps know why the ambassador might have left it out of our brief. That said, the deal does beg the question, Qig. We are strangers here on Enki; we do not even know your language; we are less than forty RIM citizens—so exactly how do you think we can help you gain the head juror position?"

It was true that the RIM had some strength here, in that they had such superior technology and knew more about governance than the Enkians. However, he wondered just what it was they could do.

The three Enkians just stared at Tanner.

Qig nodded to Tanner and those hands unclenched and opened palms up on the table.

"Captain—that, of course, is up to you. There will be the usual five candidates who will debate, then there is the election, and the results are made known. We do not know how you will do your magic. But you will do it. Or, the Fine Arts Muse will tie up the RIM Confederacy membership for as long as we have citizens to file a case, one by one, day after day ..."

Tanner frowned and looked at Qig and the others. *Was there something not being said? "So then ask," my old admiral had always said ...*

"Qig, we have almost no chance in ensuring that you are the successful candidate. You know that— so what are you not saying?" Tanner said, and he too held out his hands, palms up on the table, mirroring Qig, and waited.

"The only way that would work for sure—is if I was the only candidate," he said quietly. "As we have learned, technology eats away at our muses—

this knowledge we have learned over dozens of generations as we have seen our traditional muse beliefs require greater and greater mental defenses against threatening technology. To stay strong, we train our muse citizens to practice self-deception, to shut out contradictory evidence, and to trust our own leaders more than their own capacity to accept technology. We know that competing ideologies do not work; therefore, we choose to follow our muse. Hence, the very second-class position of our Resources and Militia Enkians. They do not matter. They do not. Hence, I cannot go to them for this—which is why we have come to you. And as you have obviously surmised, Enki needs me as the next head juror."

Tanner suspected that, but he was surprised the Enkian had come right out and said it.

We—the RIM group—are to get rid of the other candidates, so Qig is the only running Enkian for the head juror position.

Murder. Oh, it could be called something else. But that is what it was.

"Or, at least the only candidate that was a viable one. Qor of Words is the favored one, the rest are all just ballot placeholders. If he disappeared, then the job would be mine. One candidate to be ... removed. Yes, removed is the word. Can that be accomplished, Captain?"

His hands reached for each other, the fingers intertwined, the veins distended and pulsed.

Tanner nodded. He didn't know what else to do, so he nodded and then said, "Yes, that could be arranged," and his voice too was low and solemn.

Qig rose immediately, and followed by his Fine Arts Muse team, they left the room without another word.

Bram put a hand on Tanner's forearm. "Sir, one thing to note? That I am still learning how to read an Enkian—and other aliens as well—they were all very much surprised that you knew about this. And I got the feeling that the ambassador fell in their eyes for telling you about this deal. And the ending of the penalty part of same did not foretell that what they're talking about is what amounts to murder—assassination perhaps it could be called. But someone has to cut down the slate to only four candidates. And that someone is us, Sir," he said, his voice small.

Tanner nodded and sat to consider what they'd just learned. Somehow, they were to get rid of the Words Muse leader, Uigoeri Qor, by whatever means needed, so he was no longer a candidate, which would ensure Qig was elected—and the RIM Confederacy gained a new member. And the RIM also would gain access to the Enkian metal that would keep their ships safe from any kind of a ray weapon. *Big stakes*, Tanner thought, *as big as they could get.* And all he had to do was to find a way to get this all done ... and not murder anyone. Unless—and he hated adding this—there was no other way.

I could not do it myself, but I could order it, he thought as he realized he was waffling on this.

No, I couldn't do that either ... could I?

#####

Bram and Kondo looked at their captain, and both were surprised by what they'd just heard.

It was not too often that they received a PDA EYES ONLY to come to their captain's ready room STAT, but that's exactly what had happened just a few minutes ago. Tanner had taken them into his complete confidence, and they were now aware of the need to get the Enki planet into the RIM Confederacy due to the value of this new "probe metal" as it was being called. Tanner knew this news was to be kept private, but he also knew that a good captain—and he counted himself in that small group—needed to have his own confidants, and Bram and Kondo were surely that.

"That's what you need to know. I ask, of course, that this remain between us only—no one else other than the ambassador has all of this information, but it appears like it's up to us—me, I guess—to find an

149

answer. Comments, gentlemen?"

Bram deigned to Kondo who looked at Tanner with a tilted head.

"Sir, if I have this correct—and please let me know if I'm reading anything into this—but do you consider the Enkian muse society like a religion? A system of five different cults all interested in their own muse only. Is that right?" he asked, and anyone could see he didn't know if he was correct.

Tanner took a sip of tea at his desk in the captain's ready room and looked around the azure blue room. Carpeted to help keep the noise down, the room was plain with riveted bulkheads, an exterior view-port, and the captain's big desk with his console and monitors. *The tea was sweet and yet still good,* he thought. *Too bad this trip to Enki was getting so damn difficult. Probe metals versus murder. Interesting was another word too ...*

"You have my take on this, and yes, that's what I think we've blundered into here on Enki. While the muses are cults, however, I can add that at this point they appear to use their judicial system to pursue all their difficulties—not a hint at this point of any kind of cult wars or jihads. At least as far as we know so far, admittedly not the best thing to rely on," he said.

Tanner took another sip of tea. "If you think about it—cult does describe perfectly what the muses are. As we all know, having bumped into this kind of thing before. At best, the muses offer up teachings like these to discourage or even forbid the kinds of friendship and intermarriage that might help broaden a cult—where other muses or clans become a part of a larger full societal whole. At worst, outsiders or non-muse members are seen as enemies of their muse and goodness, potential agents of Satan, lacking in morality and not to be trusted. Muse believers might huddle together, anticipating martyrdom. When simmering tensions erupt, societies fracture along sectarian fault lines, and here on Enki, those fault lines are very clearly drawn."

Bram knew it was here that he had to make a decision to tell Tanner about his input testing of the Enkians and his undercover work with the Master or to keep it to himself. He made the choice not to share it yet, and he nodded and instead made a small addition to the discussion.

"Sir, we also know that they all pride themselves on their judicial system—I would doubt that there are any instances of the kind of cult vigilantism that we all worry about. So far, so good, but that still does not help our own issue with how we help to rig this election. So far, at least ..."

All three sat quietly at that point as Bram had succinctly put their own issue into a few short

151

words—how to rig an election.

No one spoke for a few minutes. Tanner sipped on his tea. Bram drank his water, and Kondo bit a fingernail.

All three knew that the probe metal was the prize and the entry fee was the rigging of the election to allow the Fine Arts Muse leader, Qig, to win the head juror position.

"We need to think on this ... and yes, as you know now, I needed help with this, and I'll tell you why. When I asked Qig what he wanted done and he explained, my immediate thoughts were murder. He wants me to kill the leader of the Words Muse, Uigoeri Qor. After more talk, while he never ever asked for that to happen, he was pretty sure that he wanted to rig the election by being the best remaining candidate. So Qor must somehow not be on the ballot. Hence, I called you in to help, figuring that three heads are better than this single old noggin."

He sipped his tea again and thought that was as honest as he could be.

He needed help—he'd lain awake now for two nights now, trying to come up with any way to get Qor off the ballot short of murder. And he'd failed.

Bram nodded and Kondo still chiseled away at that fingernail.

Neither spoke for quite a while.

Finally, fingernail defeated, Kondo spoke up. "Sir, we'll need to think on this. The election is still about three weeks away, and we need to come up with a great idea by then, but for the life of me, the only thing I can come up with right now is—well, murder, an accident, a landslide, a sandstorm— whatever the locals will buy. Sir," he said, and Tanner could tell that he too was not clear on what to do.

"Fine, let's meet up for lunch—standing orders— every day 'til we come up with a plan. I'll tell my steward and we'll have it here in my ready room daily 'til we have an answer.

"First, I would very much like to thank Stonecraw Qew for his help in arranging the transport for today," Resources head Iabisha Qed said, and he smiled at the Militia man who was seated in the Enkian shuttle back a few rows from the front. For some reason, Tanner noted, while he and Kondo had been given front row seats, there were four more rows behind them that were full of Resources members. His friend Qed was on-board at least but back several rows, and he smiled at Tanner and waved.

"We have arranged, via the ambassador's secretary, to show Captain Scott and Commander

153

Lazaro some of what the Resources section does here on Enki, so there will be a few stops along the way. First up today is a trip to a Youngling Center for you to see how Enki handles our new citizens, from hatching through to muse engagements. We are close, yes, pilot?" he asked over his shoulder and received a "Roger that" from the pilot, as the shuttle banked to port, and the brown desert below grew closer.

As the shuttle settled and Tanner looked at the big view-screen, he saw a large pyramid ahead with its telltale blue levels every so often all the way up to the summit. Unlike all the other pyramids though, he could not see an access ramp on the sands around the single pyramid. Instead, it appeared that at grade level, right off the sands, there was a large, very long doorway that was now closed.

Grade level access, he thought, *which is good because the dang steps were hard on these old knees.*

Moments later, the visitors group of more than thirty moved off the shuttle and followed the tour leaders toward that long, wide door. As they approached, it slid up in its entirety, and the noise level from within was loud. While Tanner had had little experience with children of any species, he knew that unsupervised kids got loud quickly, remembering what he'd seen back on the Hospital

Ship just a few months back. But this was louder—much louder.

The Resources leaders waved them inside, and they were immediately recognized by the hundreds of younglings inside—and the noise stopped instantly.

Amazed, Tanner looked out at the young Enkians and noted they had all stopped their play of whatever they were doing and were forming up into lines and rows. Not a word was being spoken to them or by them; it was as if this was a standard practice that occurred at times, this being one of them.

At the end of the side wall of the large rotunda area, there was a small raised dais or stage and a single Enkian stood on it. He appeared to be in charge of the hundreds of younglings in front of him, and that was a surprise at least to Tanner. One adult for hundreds of youngsters was a ratio that would mean disaster, he thought, but obviously here on Enki, it worked.

As the visitors all arrived at the dais, the Resources leader, Qed, smiled up at the Enkian on the stage. His feathered crest of black and lavender rippled with importance, and he mounted the dais. He pointed to the row of chairs arranged in front of the dais between him and the rows of younglings, and his helpers got them all seated, with Tanner and Kondo right up front.

Ahead of them, Tanner noted the younglings
were all standing and waiting for whatever came
next. Each, he could see as he inspected Enkian
youngsters for the first time, was thin and rather
awkwardly built. Not a single feather on any of
their heads had any color but white, not a single
additional color. That was odd, he thought, but it
was apparent he had much to learn about Enkian
younglings. They also wore a jumper that covered
their bodies but left those scaly legs and spurs bare.

"We welcome to Youngling Center Number Six
the RIM Confederacy representatives, Captain
Scott and Commander Lazaro, and we welcome
them with open hearts. I ask that each of you,
younglings and citizens, be as honest and as open
with our visitors as you can be ..." he finished off,
and Tanner was surprised that in front of him
hundreds and hundreds of white feathered crests
rippled in agreement.

"We have prepared a small program for you too,
so you can see what the first dozen years of a
youngling's life is like at one of our Centers," he
added.

In front of them, the rows of younglings
dissolved. The younglings reformed in a squared
U-shape. A group of eleven younglings took the
empty center of the square, moved up closer to the

dais and the seated visitors, and took up their positions.

Moments later, music sounded throughout the huge rotunda, and the eleven began to dance—at least that was what it looked like. The music had a driving sort of rhythm, and they stamped their feet in the same tempo, their arms twisting in time. It appeared that there was nothing more than that dance to celebrate, as nothing else happened for more than five minutes. At the end, the eleven younglings formed a row across the top of the U shape, forming a square, and bowed as a unit. The seated visitors applauded, and Tanner noted all the fluttering feathered crests among the younglings.

After the Dance Muse presentation, the visitors sat through the Words Muse presentation. Eleven pieces of all kinds of scripts and humor and drama were read. Tanner didn't get the humor but noted many of the Enkians roared with laughter. After the Words Muse presentation, the Music Muse presentation came, and those eleven youngling musicians played instruments Tanner had never seen before though some looked violin-like. The actual work they played ran a bit longer than others, but Tanner rather enjoyed it—it was a cross between what he'd call a college football fight song and a funeral dirge. How they merged, he had no idea, but he liked their works. He clapped loudly and longer than most.

The Performance Muse presentation was next, and the visitors were treated with an act from a larger work. It looked interesting, though why some of the Enkian younglings were hiding under furniture was beyond him. Fine Arts Muse offered a simple look at how their muse was courted—each of the eleven younglings worked on their art for their short performance. Some painted, some carved in marble, and others worked in clay. It too received a large applause to end the five muse presentations.

"We Resources section leaders would like to thank the staff here at Youngling Center Number Six for their hard work in the planning and presentation of the program today. We would also like to thank the fifty-five younglings who presented too and would offer that they are surely going to excel at the upcoming graduation day next week, which is Enki-wide. Dismissed, younglings," he said, and the room exploded with younglings, noisy, running, and traipsing all over.

Tanner rose as did Kondo, and they stood with the others. Tanner waved Stonecraw Qew over to them.

"This was great, so good to see, Stonecraw. My thanks for this to you, and please pass that along to the Resources team too, never seen anything like it!"

he said, and he was being as honest as he could be. It had been interesting, although it made him want to ask a whole host of further questions.

Later on the Enkian shuttle back to their home base on Enki, the capital city, he sat with the Resources leader, Iabisha Qed, asked his questions, and received answers that made him sit back and ponder.

CHAPTER FIVE

The *CN Pollux* winked back into normal space a little more than a half light year from Enki and immediately went to full Impulse power in an attempt to get to its goal, which was to get to the planet as soon as possible.

Captain Abu al-Hasan turned to his XO and said, "Scan for RIM ships, please, XO—and if you see any Enki ships too, let me know soonest."

His Ramat XO smiled and nodded as he stared at his console and began to flip buttons and toggles as his scans went out. The *Pollux* was a Caliphate ship, a full destroyer that went along at two lights a day, and they'd just pulled into the Enki area on a major rush trip from Halberd. They'd been sent here on an emergency basis by the Caliph and had orders to be the first of many RIM ships to come. "And yes, they'd been first," al-Hasan said to himself.

As the ship moved towards high orbit, they were immediately challenged by the *Atlas* via Ansible, and the captain said to ignore the messages that they needed to check in and the planet was no-contact according to RIM statutes. And they drew closer.

The Ansible stopped buzzing, and they still cruised on at top speed.

A full five minutes later, the XO spoke up with a hint of urgency in his voice. "Sir, long-range sensors report that there are missiles inbound—ETA of three minutes. Not known what they're carrying but can't be good, Sir," he said as his hands still flew over his console.

Abu al-Hasan sat for a moment in his captain's chair and then he sighed.

He nodded to his Ansible officer, and they placed a call in to the *Atlas*, which was answered but only after a full minute went by.

Appearing on the *Pollux's* main view-screen, Captain Tanner Scott was busy with something and didn't pay attention to the new connection for a bit, and al-Hasan finally had to speak.

"Captain Scott, have you launched missiles to greet a RIM Confederacy member ship? You do realize that I will have to report this affront to a full Confederacy member by just another member—

you're not in the RIM Navy anymore, Scott."

"Oh, not entirely, Captain. The *Atlas* has been the nominated RIM Navy vessel for this member candidate mission for almost two months. The Caliphate knows that like the rest of the Confederacy. The missiles, which are still on their way, were automatically launched to intercept an intruder. Soon as we verify that you are who you say you are, we'll call them back. XO, any issues with verification?" Scott said to someone off screen, and a few seconds later, he nodded.

"We've recalled them, Captain. Take up a high orbit near us, please, and then come over to see me via shuttle. You are not allowed to set down on-planet either under any circumstances. You have been instructed, and we will not stop any further missiles. End conn," he said, and the view-screen went to black.

"May Allah damn his drunken soul," the XO of the *Pollux* said loudly, and the comment received nods and sounds of agreement all across the *Pollux's* bridge. All the crew agreed with that, and yet they also knew the Barony Navy captain was correct.

No one was allowed to set down on Enki on their own, as the diplomatic mission was still in progress. Anyone was allowed to orbit, but they had to check in first. And they'd been caught, but good. So now, they had to play a different kind of game to get down to the planet and see what they could do to find access to the probe metal on their own—for the Caliphate. They had a mission, and if you were in the Caliphate, you understood what would happen should you fail.

#####

Tanner knew most of the information Gallipedia presented on the UrPoPoi. The UrPoPoi were a bipedal species and were generally considered to be "humanoid" despite numerous pronounced anatomical differences. They were shorter than humans of average height and had slender bodies. Their faces were characterized by large, bulging eyes, pronounced lips, and a lack of any protruding nasal structure. They were omnivores, feeding mostly on plants and mollusks. And because the UrPoPoi skin was very sensitive to changes in humidity and quickly dried out, they preferred to spend as much of their time as possible in or near water and away from the sun. On their heads, they had the faintest of what might be called feathers but so tiny as to be almost un-noticeable.

Dryness of the skin was extremely painful and even dangerous to an UrPoPoi, and they quickly succumbed to the effects of dehydration. Their natural habitats included shallow river deltas, swamps, and rain forests.

After confirming what he knew about the
UrPoPoi in Gallipedia, Tanner was even more
surprised by the story that the Enkians were
descendants of the UrPoPoi. According to the
story, more than ten thousand years ago, the
UrPoPoi had found Enki and moved a small
colony there. It was beyond belief to imagine the
Enkians had evolved from the UrPoPoi with the
UrPoPoi's climate requirements, intolerance of
sunlight, and need for water.

Tanner knew the UrPoPoi never went to hot
planets like Enki, and yet, here they were, as the
UrPoPoi ship the *UN Andiya* dropped out of light
speed and took up a picket position with the rest of
the RIM group of ships that lay above Enki in low
orbit.

Lieutenant Irving, the *Atlas* Ansible officer, had
told him there was going to be a communal
Ansible, and they had been invited as a blind copy
so they could hear the conversation but not be seen
by the UrPoPoi side.

He nodded to instruct his lieutenant to comply,
and in a few moments, the big view-screen was lit
up with the face of the UrPoPoi caller, whose name
on the sidebar was Ambassador Nathan Ritchie.

He had no nose and the big bulging eyes, a
mixture of black and brown with no white at all

that he could see dominated his face. His protruding lips looked very wet with saliva or something like that, he thought. The ambassadors was pitted and looked damp with large pores that perhaps held water or sweat or some kind of liquid. All in all, an alien, he thought, that looked just a bit out of place on a planet that was more than a hundred degrees at midnight. *This might be interesting*, he thought, and he sat back like the rest of his bridge crew to see what the UrPoPoi wanted.

"What we want, Mr. Ambassador, is for you to verify with your watchdogs up here in orbit that we —our small UrPoPo diplomatic team—can come down by shuttle to speak to you directly, in person, on this whole RIM membership fiasco. We want to make our presentation in person, Ambassador Harmon—from one diplomat to another, Sir."

The UrPoPo ambassador certainly knew his way around diplomacy, and Ambassador Harmon granted his request. Tanner nodded to Lieutenant Irving, as he watched the Ansible meeting.

"Go to private, please, XO," he said, and the UrPoPoi feed was put on mute and a direct-in connection formed to the ambassador only.

"Captain Scott, please allow the one UrPoPo shuttle to transport down to the current RIM offices here in the Words Muse pyramid. I would like there to be no more than a dozen, let's say, of them, and I will make that known to them. But also be very aware, Captain, that you monitor their ship and any other in-out traffic too, please. Let me know immediately via private EYES ONLY to my PDA, please, should that occur."

Their ambassador turned away from the screen, and it went to black.

Tanner looked over at Kondo, his XO, and smiled.

"So UrPoPo weighs in—they should'a been here a month ago, I figure," he said, and he looked for an answer from his XO.

Kondo nodded. "Sir, they surely have an arguable case—they sit one orbit away from the same sun as Enki; the Enkians have been trading partners for them for over a thousand years; they offer up some specialized products to them—fine marble, I'm told, and a host of other art supplies. But they did nothing. We've been here almost five weeks and they—well, as far as I know—have never even contacted us let alone the Enkians to offer up their own sponsorship to a full RIM Confederacy membership. Personally, I think that's odd—or maybe they know something we don't—yet here they are, today. And the fact that they'd dry up and fade away in five minutes down on Enki obviously hasn't affected their wants to get in on the talks."

Tanner nodded and they talked on the topic for a while.

"Sir, shuttle away from the *UN Drastic*, and there are ... only eleven life signs onboard. Oh, one is not an UrPoPoi but a human. No idea who though at this point, Sir," the *Atlas* helm officer, Lieutenant Cooper said. His hands flew on his console, and from quite a few feet away, Tanner could see some flashing icons.

"Sir, a quick look shows us that whomever this human is, their heartbeats are raised, breathing elevated too. Seems that whomever it is, they are anxious about this trip or nervous about the Enkians—no way to tell that, Sir," Cooper added, and that got him a nod and a "Nicely done, young man" from his captain.

"On screen, please" Tanner said, and he and the rest of the bridge crew watched as the UrPoPoi shuttle slowly wheeled away from its mother ship and moved down toward the planet.

Against the huge swaths of brown desert, the bright blue shuttle slowly dropped away from the low orbit position, receding and getting smaller all the time. In less than a few minutes, it disappeared down into the atmosphere and was gone.

"Sir," his XO said, "should we track the disembarking of the diplomatic team?"

"Yes, please," said Tanner, and he sat back to sip

on his fresh tea. Not a double-double but not too bad. He grinned and recalled some of his past remembrances of the bridge on the *Atlas* and the *Marwick* too. He could remember spilling coffee on his uniform shirt and retiring to his quarters to get a fresh shirt and a double of Scotch added to his coffee. He remembered hiding a bottle in his ready room or down in the gym on Deck Twenty-three or getting his steward to add it to his dinner glass surreptitiously. He shook his head. He thought he'd been hiding his addiction, but everyone seemed to know. Of course, getting totally lit up like a spotlight didn't help, and many of the old crew knew and had helped him hide it. And while he'd been sent to the RIM prison planet to try to get rid of that addiction, that had been bypassed by the convict revolt and his help in putting down that riot. The fact that he'd had to kill two of the rioters —one whom he actually liked a lot, a woman named Tibah, was not important to the memory, Tanner thought, as he noticed his hands were both still. He had to do what he had to do; it was called attention to duty. Still no fingers tapping, he noted. But the events on Halberd had been followed with his resignation from the RIM Navy and accepting the captaincy in the Barony Navy—and the care and control of the *Atlas*.

He smiled. He'd just run through the past few

years, and there was no PTSD rearing its head right now.

That was worth the smile. But he also knew there was a difference between running over a recent memory and being under stress and having those memories come storming back into his consciousness.

"So far," he said to himself, "so good ..."

#####

Tanner sat in the Officers' Mess and swirled the Scotch around in the rocks glass in front of him. Alone at a side booth, he let the glass sit now, picked up his juice, and took a swig of that for now. He'd been here for over an hour and was on his second juice, but the same Scotch sat in front of him, untouched.

He leaned back, stretched out one of his long legs, and wondered why designers in the food-service world always made the dang booths so cramped..

Never enough room for us six footers.

Hell, even that's a lie 'cause I'm only five feet eleven inches tall. So the designer here should be demoted to designing Garnuthian pigsties. He smiled even wider, slid down a little on his bench, and looked back at the glass of Scotch.

His admiral had called him not two hours ago—

well, his ex-admiral to be exact. It had been an
EYES ONLY request, which he had ducked at first
but then grudgingly accepted in his ready room. He
had sat there for a full ten minutes trying to hit the
accept button and failed every time he reached
forward. But eventually, the flashing icon won out,
and he had steeled himself to accept the call. The
two of them had decades of history together. The
EYES ONLY conversation with the admiral
replayed in Tanner's mind as he stared at the Scotch
in front of him.

The admiral stared at him for a full minute before
he finally spoke.

"Captain Scott, good of you to take my call," he
said, his voice somber.

The admiral was—or rather had been—a friend, a
mentor, and someone who had saved his life a few
times when years ago they had been in the Earl of
Kinross's Navy to inward. McQueen had been the
admiral who had repelled an alien attack, and
Tanner had captained a ship that aided in that war.
After that and the huge costs that such a victory
had cost them both, they had left and went outward
toward the RIM. That had taken years and Sleeper
Ship time, but they had ended up here on the RIM,
in the RIM Navy.

Admiral McQueen ran the RIM Navy, and
under him, Tanner had taken on an XO role on the

Navy frigate the *Kerry*. Attacked by pirates, their captain killed, Tanner had stepped up with his well-honed combat tactics, had defeated those pirates, and had earned a full captaincy on the *Marwick* in the RIM Navy. Of course, his alcoholism grew as did his rank, and he ended up loaded and had embarrassed the Navy as well as his admiral.

Resigning his captaincy back on Halberd, the RIM prison planet, and moving over to the Barony Navy had happened soon after, and then the cure for alcoholism had happened recently over on the Barony Hospital Ship. It hadn't been tested, he knew, but his general practitioner and his psychiatrist had both verified that he had had the treatment and would never ever be drunk again. No matter how much he drank, the alcohol would be disregarded by his body, sluiced out directly into his urine. And if there was no lift from the booze, it was argued, then why bother, they said.

Tanner carried this around in his head, and he knew that he owed his admiral something, but what?

He nodded to Admiral McQueen and one hand drew little circles on his ready room desk. The other, he was beating out that one, two ... one, two ... pattern on his right knee below the desktop.

"Sir, yes, how may I help you—or the RIM Navy

even?" he said.

The admiral looked down at some papers in front of him on his console and then back up at Tanner. "There appears to be a rising argument made here on Juno at the Executive Committee level that something is going wrong with our—with your— attempts to get the Enkians to accept membership in the RIM Confederacy. At least that is what we hear from our Master Adept. And I wanted to contact you directly—to ask you personally, for you to watch over these negotiations as closely as you can. To read what you can of their strengths as a force that we may one day face in the field. And lastly, to see if you get a sense of what kind of an adversary the Enkians would be—should that ever arise, Captain," he said.

Tanner was not surprised that the conversation had been steered to the content of the call itself— rather than anything of a personal note between them.

He indicated that yes, he would surely get back to the admiral with a wrap-up report to include any recon that would help the RIM Navy in the future. He had also admitted that he would be sending the same report to his Barony Captains Council as well as the Baroness too. That was a part of his duty as a Barony Navy officer. The admiral would know that.

He smiled at the admiral and signed off without any kind of a personal note either.

Finished replaying the EYES ONLY communication with the admiral in his mind, Tanner swirled the Scotch around in the glass now, and he wondered what he might have said, could have said, or should have said, and he came up empty. There was really very little to say, he thought, and that was because, perhaps, there was far too much to say.

That might still happen sometime in the future.

"But not now," he said to himself, as he tossed the Scotch down his throat, and catching the eye of the steward, he ordered another double.

More than an hour after that, and after seven doubles, he felt nothing.

Not a blessed rise in temperature, no extra sweating, no increased breathing either. There were no clues when it came to his body.

He was sober as far as he could tell. The damage that seven Scotch doubles should do to his normal attitude and demeanor was high, he knew. But whatever had been in the shot he'd had a few months back on the Barony Hospital Ship had worked so far.

Course, he thought, *maybe that wasn't enough ... or maybe it was.* His last attempt to find that bucolic alcohol high, which he now knew he would no longer find, was done.

He smiled at himself, and with his juice, he toasted the doctors on the Hospital Ship who had obviously known what they were doing.

The fleeting thought that he had tried to get drunk after failing to face his mentor, the admiral, came to him.

And he threw it away because he knew that out here on the RIM, there would always be a chance to see the admiral again.

Penance is as penance does, he thought.

Uigoeri Qor, leader of Words Muse, rose in the negotiations room and addressed the large group before him.

On one side of the horseshoe table sat the five leaders of the Words Muse, along with a few aides and assistants. On the other, the RIM ambassador and his larger group of minions sat, and all had their eyes on Qor as he looked around the room. Sitting against the far wall were representatives from the Resources and Militia groups along with a single Enkian from the other four muses, Dance, Fine Arts, Music, and Performance. And on the opposite wall were the seats that held the RIM Navy, Barony Navy, and Duchy Navy officers who again were there for support. These negotiation room visitors were just that—they could take no part in the talks, but the negotiating team at the table could call upon them for help or counsel or advice.

Not that it had happened, Tanner thought, *since we've been here.*

Negotiations had been moving along pretty well, he thought, but then again, he had nothing to measure that by.

They had left some of the tougher items alone at this point, and instead they had so far worked out a large majority of minor points. Trade for agricultural imports and exports, manufacturing, technology and its incoming impact were big items. But all had been handled to the satisfaction of both sides and signed off on, and they had moved to the next item.

Tanner knew that mining and refining would be coming up very soon, and that was of major interest for the RIM group as the probe metal would be a part of that area too. *Course,* he thought, *we won't be spelling out any interest at all in that metal, just ensuring that it would be included in the overall classifications that would be agreed to later.*

Qor looked at them all once more and held out his hands. His talons were very polished and shiny. With a hint that he was not so happy to be saying the words, Qor said, "I am sorry, but I have to announce that we are going to have to suspend our negotiations on our RIM membership candidacy for the time being," he said.

And that got a whirl of comments from the diplomats in the front row of the seats of the table.

"Wait—" Ambassador Harmon said.

"We do not have the time—" another diplomat said.

"Certainly not, this is not the way that—" a third diplomat said.

Holding up both hands, palms facing the RIM side of the table, Qor went on.

"Yes, I know that this sounds odd—but you must know that we are breaking off talks for only the next two weeks. Other items have occurred that require our—my—immediate attention, and I am sorry, but to do these negotiations justice, I cannot spare the time at present," he said, and then he sat down heavily at his place.

Directly opposite him, Ambassador Harmon rose and held out a hand to quiet his own team.

"Might we know what these other items are, please, Qor, so that we can understand this delay? We know that you, like the RIM, are wanting to keep our negotiations ongoing and moving forward. Can I ask that, at the least, please?" he said and then he sat.

Qor nodded and rose. "Yes, that is proper too, we

feel. For your information, as we are the lead muse
—Words Muse, I mean—as we are the lead muse
on the next graduation day event to be held right
here in our pyramid, the time for that is a major
drain up until it happens next week," he said and
then he sat.

Tanner thought they should have agreed long ago
they could be seated when they spoke to each other,
as his ambassador rose once again.

"But that is only a week away—so may we also
then schedule to reconvene, say, one week from
tomorrow?" he asked very politely and sat down
once more.

Rising, the Enkian shook his head. "I also must
inform you that there will be an election held one
week later for the head juror position, as the current
leader, Iavoesi Qax, will be retiring. And in that
election, I am running for that position. Which does
mean that should I be successful, then the seat here
in the negotiations room will be held by someone
else," he said as he pointed at the other four leaders
of the Words Muse.

"It could be one of these fine leaders, or even my
replacement, whomever that might be. But in any
case, it means that my time will be spent on the
election process—so we need at least two weeks in
our delay timeline. There can be nothing else done,"
he said, and he sat down again.

Tanner knew all of this, but it was good to have it out in the open now.

If Qor were successful, they'd be dealing with someone else as the Words Muse leader.

If he failed in his election, then he'd be back in that same chair, so as far as any concerns, negotiations would then happen.

All good to know, but then the ambassador rose.

"Qor, we are most pleasantly happy for you and your attempt to gain the head juror's position, and while we are outsiders here, if there is anything that we can do to help, please just ask," he said and he sat.

Everyone was still seated and as talks had just been put on hold, they all rose to leave.

Tanner grabbed Stonecraw Qew's arm as they left the room and walked down the short corridor to the huge rotunda area at the base of the Words Muse pyramid.

"So, we've a couple of weeks off—maybe you could arrange for a trip to your technology centers or your spaceport—that's an area we'd like to see," he said.

Stonecraw Qew nodded. "I will personally call my conda to ask, but that should not be a problem," he said, and they left the pyramid together.

CHAPTER SIX

As the tank technician slowly worked his way down the long row of cryonic tanks, he noticed no one had swept or mopped up the floor ahead and off to port. Something had leaked but he was positive it was not a single tank in this—his—row. He had been doing this now for six months, since the *SN Majestic* had left her last port on Lambda 4 and sailed for the RIM. Every day, the same thing, and that made him a happy technician.

"Nothing to think about, nothing changing every day. Set standard operating procedures, the kind of thing that anyone with a brain would want. And the job was his," he said to himself and smiled.

Ahead at the next two tanks, he turned to his right first and looked at the display screen as the standard monitoring of a sleeper began.

179

Male, Seenra race, fifty-nine years, normal range of O_2, vitals all within range, and interior gas levels at optimum. Injected chemicals were also within range.

"No surprises here," he said to himself, as he picked up his tablet off his cart and tapped it against the display screen to transfer the vitals from the sleeper tank over to his tablet for eventual upload to the ship's sleeper monitoring database.

"Next," he said to himself, and he turned around, pushed the cart a few feet closer to the matching tank on this row, and stopped cold.

He was standing in some kind of fluid, and it had no odor or color. *Like water*, he thought. The shallow puddle had spread across the floor tread plates, and it was the same fluid he'd seen a couple of tanks back.

He looked at the monitor and noted that all looked well. *Wait, what's this?* A flashing icon reported a low level of interior fluids. While the sleeper was not completely covered by liquid in their cryonic tank, there was a small volume of water in each tank of about knee depth, which was used to moderate the interior temperature levels. Liquids worked best, it had been found decades ago, to keep the sleeper in the most viable range of temperatures.

And this level was low, the icon indicated.

He nodded and did not smile. This was the first issue he'd run into since the ship had left Lambda 4, and it bothered him that this issue with a tank and it's seals, most likely, would be on his report. He made a note on his tablet and then clicked the icon on the monitor to stop the flashing.

The repair request would go to engineering. They'd schedule a repair technician to come down, pop the tank to make a change to the seals, and see if that fixed the issue.

Meanwhile, he looked at the monitor to check on the occupant of the faulty tank.

Female, human race, twenty-six years, normal range of O_2, vitals all at low range but still acceptable, interior gas a little thin but still okay, and injected chemicals were fine. He tapped his tablet to copy over the vital statistics for later upload and noted the name of the occupant too—one Gia Scott of Branton in the Earldom of Kinross. He added in the repair request note that the sleeper had vitals that were all at the low or thin edge of their ranges. He ensured that he clicked the top priority category for the message and clicked send.

He stepped out of the puddle slowly hating that the bottoms of his clean shoes were now wet. When he got back out on the main walkway, he stamped his shoes to get the water off, and he was only partially successful.

As he worked his way down to the next duo of facing tanks, he left wet partial footprints behind him on the floor tread plates.

He hated changes and hoped the tank that was leaking was adjusted soon—before the tank occupant was affected more, he hoped.

#####

There was no doubt that the room was plain and had been plain for over a generation, the Baroness said to herself. "Yet there are now at least some items that added a dash of style, of color, and yes, even some Executive Committee panache too!" She looked over at the far wall, which was made of brick and saw a native Ikarian carving out of some kind of wood they had found on Throth. The Ikarians had used their skills to create what looked like a huge feathered serpent. *The swirling colors of its feathers painted with bright oranges and reds on the yellow skin of the snake with blue eyes added a real whoop of color,* she thought.

Looking to her left, she saw the solid wall of bookcases. The middle four rows on each column had been emptied and cleaned, and there were now sculptures from Bottle, knick-knacks from Ttseen, and carvings of real sailing ships from DenKoss. These items came from her gift room where the gifts that had been presented to her and her late husband had been stored, which her aide had retrieved for her.

She remembered going way down a long wing in her palace and having to take two different elevators down to a sub-basement somewhere to even find the room. Thank God, an aide had already made the trip and could show her where to go. Once she went into the long room, she was amazed at what she saw. Industrial-grade shelving, thousands of feet in length, held everything from a fully stuffed Jael, the huge bearlike creature from the Duchy world of Anulet, to a set of twenty-four perfectly matched Quaran wine glasses that supposedly cost a king's ransom each. There was so much more that she walked the rows, looking and oohing and aahing. There were so many items she'd never even seen before, probably from her late husband. When she asked, the aide had no idea but confirmed she'd check the palace database to find out—but she added that this room was only one of three here in the sub-basement and the gifts had been coming for many, many Barons and Baronesses over the past thousand years.

That made her think about her past and then her future, and a second later, she shrugged.

She instructed her aide to take a wide selection of items on a specialized trip to Juno, to the Navy Hall building, and to make sure they picked a wide assortment from across the RIM. Not just Barony items, she had been insistent but items from all over the Confederacy. At least a single item from all forty of the Confederacy member realms, she cautioned. And judging by the number of items she saw now, the aide had done well. While some looked familiar, she had no idea where dozens of them had come from. She couldn't place windmill made out of some kind of crystal as coming from the RIM. She also didn't recognize the spinning top which seemed to spin, then slow to almost nothing, and then speed back up on its own. There were whole rows that she was lost on, but one thing was for sure, there was some branding here of the various Confederacy realms. And yes, she recognized the other six realms that had a member here on the Executive Council, the administrative arm of the full Council.

She waited as she'd come early today to double-check the changes she'd requested had been done. A moment later, the admiral, leader of the RIM Navy, bustled in, and finding her there early, he stopped in surprise.

"Baroness, how nice to see you so prompt," he said dryly, and he dropped his double handful of files and folders and sat heavily in his chair. As the head of the RIM Navy, he had a spot here at the table and, yes, even a full voting position, but he seldom if ever disagreed with the consensus around the table. Admiral McQueen, a human man of about eighty years or so, was in his prime. His reputation as both a strategic and tactical leader was known all across the RIM and inward for more than two thousand lights. *We are lucky to have him,* she thought. *If only he wasn't so hard to manage.* She knew he had been and would be a major competitor for her and the Barony.

"Admiral, yes, good to see you too. I was here early to check on our new surroundings, and I'm happy for the most part," she said and waved a hand at the new decor.

He nodded and yet didn't even look up as he arranged his folders into piles and grunted as if to agree with her.

She toyed with her tablet at her station at the round table with chairs for the seven Executive Committee members. As she turned and looked behind her out the window on the top floor of Navy Hall, she noticed it had gotten a bit cloudy outside and the sunlight was patchy looking down on the grass in front of the building. On the road out front, she saw a couple of limos parked, which meant more members of the Committee were probably on their way up. Just as she thought that, the doorway filled with bodies.

First came the Master Adept, the woman who

was the head of the Issian race, who lived out on
Eons, a RIM member, and she nodded to both her
and the Admiral as she took her seat. She was
followed quickly by the Caliph of the Nerian
Caliphate, the chairman of Alex'n, the doge of
Conclusion, and finally the duke of the Duchy of
d'Avigdor. *All here and accounted for,* the Baroness
thought, *and that's at least a start.*

Chairman Gramsci smiled at them all, and with
two of his hands, he arranged his tablet in front of
him on the tabletop. Two more hands sorted the
contents of a file folder while his last two tucked
themselves into his waistband on his trousers, and
he looked at the printed Agenda in front of him.

"This will not be a long meeting—unlike, I might
add, the last one with the whole Faraway trade war
discussion. Note please, that I called it a discussion
—not a shouting match, which it also was. In any
event, we start today with that situation, and the
admiral will speak on that first. Admiral McQueen,
you have the floor," he finished off and leaned back.

McQueen keyed something on his tablet, and the
big view-screen on the other brick wall lit up. "As
we expected, the trade wars between Faraway and
the Leudis took a turn for the worse—seen by the
way by our own Master Adept. I will be the first to
admit that I did doubt that the war would ever
erupt into violence as we were forewarned, but it

did happen. Leudis over on Quaran were attacked by a squad of Faraway marines, at a local wine show there. There were no casualties, but the Quarans levied some large fines and penalties against the Faraway ship that were unpaid. So they sent, it seems, a larger force to 'get' those fees paid to Faraway itself and sanctioned all trade with Faraway until those penalties were paid. Met off Faraway by one of their cruisers, they had no choice but to turn back or else there would have been a battle right there and then. Soon as the Leudis got that information, they plastered that whole part of the RIM with the news about the sanctions and began to offer to take over contracts that as of then couldn't be fulfilled. That got the Faraway world in a tizzy, and we sent in the frigate the *Kerry*, the cruisers *Marwick* and *Altair,* and our big destroyer the *Nugent* too," he said as he paused.

"And that didn't do it either," the Baroness said to herself.

"As we expected, that didn't seem to be enough firepower on our side, but it must have been seen as that by Faraway. They claim that they have lost more than twelve percent of their GDP based on the contracts that they say were stolen by the Leudis. We have no way to check on that at this point, but we are trying to get some solid estimates. In any event, this all comes to the full RIM Council next month for adjudication—and the Faraway member is screaming for blood."

There were a series of nods around the table, and it was agreed to hold a special meeting later this evening with that being the only topic of discussion. The chairman made some notes with a few hands and then moved on.

"On Enki, we have a small issue—and I want it to not become another shouting match either. While Ambassador Harmon is working on the negotiations, and we all know how important that is with us wanting Enki to become a full member so that we can all gain access to what's being called"— he stopped as he looked down at a page in front of him—"umm ... probe metal, it appears is its name, I would gather. While the diplomatic meetings have been put on hold for two weeks more, while local events unfurl, what the issue is, is this. There have been three RIM members who have taken a low orbit position and might be attempting to sway the talks or intervene in some way," he said quietly.

She knew the answer before she asked the question, but that was a tactical move she'd learned long ago.

"And who are those three members, Chairman?"

He looked directly at the Caliph. "First up is the Caliphate, then the UrPoPo contingent, and finally a Faraway frigate too. All three have taken up orbit, as I said, and then asked to land, and all three were refused by the ambassador. Up in orbit, we have the *Atlas* from the Barony and the *Triumph* from the Duchy too, all ably captained, and yes, both under the control of Ambassador Harmon." He stopped and all heads turned to the Caliph.

"We, like two of you here, are simply taking up picket duty to see what happens and yes, if the probe metal can be salvaged no matter how the diplomacy works out. We sit like everyone else is all we are doing," the Caliph said in such a way that they believed him.

At least most did, the Baroness thought.

The chairman nodded. "Further, yes ... there are some further developments, but I cannot share those at this point on instruction from the ambassador, but he says not to worry, talks are going well. There is a real bond developing between him and the Enkians, and we may expect a good outcome, fingers crossed, he noted," the chairman said as yet another set of hands made notes on his tablet and he looked back at his Agenda.

"Next item, the outstanding tax rebates on Skogg and Conclusion—perhaps the doge might like to start with this one," he said.

#####

Stonecraw Qew moved down the corridor and then over to a hidden set of stairs. As he did, he grinned back at Bram and went down a side corridor to the left. As he entered a double set of doors, he moved off to one side immediately.

The noise level was up, there was a large amount of movement, and the whole place looked sanitary and secure.

It looks like a food processing automated production line, Bram thought. *But one of huge proportions.*

From one side of the room, a conveyor belt trucked in those round small bites of food — *the consistency of a sponge sort of*, he thought. Each was about the size of a golf ball and was pure white. Thousands and thousands of them went by on the huge belt, all to make curve after curve and then end up in a straight row that made its way to the center of the room.

Bram watched, as at that center node, there was a huge set of tanks, tubes, and spay jets that hung down from the ceiling. They were big, yet they all looked the same, rising up and through the ceiling. *Going God knows where*, Bram thought.

As he was led by Stonecraw Qew to that central node and then up the short stairs to that level, Bram saw one Enkian wearing, of course, the black and lavender colors of the Resources section. His feathered crest was wilted a bit because, Bram was sure, he was at work. And what was that work, he wondered, and had the answer almost in an instant from Stonecraw Qew.

"This is Resources Officer Swanki, and it is his job to be the technician who handles our chem treating of the food here at the Words Muse pyramid. It is up to him to—well, not really up to him as he follows the lights on his console—to decide which food pellets to treat with which chems. Some, as you would assume, would carry the colors of the Words Muse of red and white; others for all of the other four varieties. Officer Swanki, can you find a minute to chat with us— Lieutenant Sander and I?" Stonecraw Qew said nicely.

As Bram watched, Officer Swanki pushed a couple of buttons on the console in front of him and the whole line stopped. He turned to face Bram and the militia officer and smiled at them. "Lieutenant, so nice to have you drop by—normally it's months between any kind of visitors we get down here. What can I tell you about what it is we do here?" He smiled once more.

Clearly someone has let this techie know that he's to be nice to me—and isn't that special, Bram thought.

"Well, can you begin telling me what it is you do —and why it's an important part of the Resources section works?" He smiled at the Enkian and leaned on the shoulder-high railing that lay between where they were standing and the neat rows of food bites on the conveyor line.

"Our job is pretty easy really, Lieutenant. What happens here is that way down there," he said as he pointed off to the left side of this huge room, "these food bites are all loaded, tray by tray, onto the conveyor belt. As the belt is on automatics, it moves them all by this single chemical imprinting station here—this large metal enclosure." He pointed directly in front of him. As the trays fed in from the left, they disappeared beneath the shroud of what he'd called the imprinting station to reappear ten feet farther down the conveyor belt.

"It's here that the station, having been preset by myself, imprints each of the food bites or pellets with a specialized chemical spray. For the Words Muse, their earmarked food pellets get the chemicals that will color their feathered crests with their muse colors of red and white. Militia gets blue and red on tan stripes, Performance gets its own purple and orange, and so on. Each of the seven different groups of Enkians gets their own—and only their own—chemically imprinted food bites because eating same causes their feathers to turn to that muse coloration. Simple. Neat and can't be messed up, we've found over the past generations," he finished off, and Bram could tell the tech was pleased with himself and his work.

Pointing over the Enkian's shoulder, Bram asked, "And over there, behind this automatic conveyor system?"

The Enkian turned, nodded, and looked through the glass wall that lay between them and the rest of the sealed off room. Back there, it looked like there were seven large liquid pools, all covered with a grid of bars, like an open grating lid. On top of those lids sat seven tall carts, each with a grid of open cage walls and tops. Inside, Bram could see more of these food bites, and yet these were somehow being treated differently.

"Ah, the younglings' injections. Yes, as you know, our younglings on their graduation are all sorted into either one of the five muses or the Resources or Militia sections. And all of them have pure white feathered crests. The food bites you see here behind us are all in racks of cages sitting over their specific muse pool. When I engage the system, each of those lids on the pools will descend taking down their own racks of food bites. Because the bites will be totally immersed in their chemical bath, and left there for five minutes to be totally potent, they turn the feathered crests for those younglings in one overnight session. A youngling goes into their graduation and wakes up with their muse's colors draped all over their crest. It's pretty special and is

193

one of the wonders on Enki. As a Resources tech, I
know all about it. I push a button and a bit later, the
food bites are ready to be consumed. So tomorrow
when I start my shift, the button will be pushed and
the process begun," he finished off and smiled even
more broadly.

"If he could pat himself on the back, he surely
would," Bram said to himself, nodded, and smiled
back.

He drilled down inside the man's head and
looked for deception and there was none. *He is what
he appears to be.*

He looked next for any kind of shading or
embellishment and again there was none.

He looked lastly for anything else—and that's
when he noticed one thing, which made him smile
even more.

The complete description of the injection process
that the Enkian had just delivered to him had been
from his training. He had never ever done such a
procedure himself, as he relied on his training,
which meant that for him to implement that
procedure, all he needed to do was push a button
on his operator's console.

Bram put the thought of which button that was
forward in the Enkian's mind and watched as the
thought took hold. The tech moved his hand to the
top orange button on the far right side of the

console keyboard. It was under a clear lid that would need to be lifted up first, Bram noted, but that was the button the whole process linked to—and that made Bram's smile as broad as the Resources tech's smile, and they grinned at each other.

This was not missed by Stonecraw, and he thanked the tech for his time and ushered Bram back down the walkway to the stairs that led up to the ground level in the Resources pyramid. He led the way over to the exterior doors and pushed through and out onto the sand.

The Resources pyramid sat in the middle of the other five muse pyramids, as each of those required direct access for their own resources, and this was the standard formation for all pyramid cities on Enki. He struck out across the sands, the heat rising so quickly that they both began to sweat before they'd gone twenty feet. Bram caught up with him and held out a hand to stop him.

"Stonecraw, is there something wrong?" he asked, wondering if his mind reading a few minutes ago had been found out.

The Militia man looked down at his feet, half buried in the sands, and flipped some of the sand off one foot as he flexed one of those huge toes, the talon spraying sands in a half-circle.

"Not really, no ... it's just that you seemed to

make a friend there with that tech so easily—and I didn't want you to think that a Resources section Enkian should be that close to you. You are a RIM group member, and we—the Militia—are responsible for you and the rest of the group. Probably just my way of thinking, but I am charged with the duty to protect whomever I accompany, and I'd rather be safe than sorry, Bram. Sorry, nothing else but that," he said, and they both continued to walk across the sands.

Odd, Bram thought, *that the Enkian Militia man felt that he should not only protect us against any kind of injury but also against any kind of friendship too. That was very odd ...*

#####

The Baroness threw the whole sheaf of papers across her desk at one of her accountants and then pointed at the woman. "I shall have you beheaded! Don't forget that I can do just that, little Miss Bean Counter. How dare you bring me such a spreadsheet with those bloody God-awful numbers and projections? You should lose your license to practice, you fool!" she sputtered and went to stare out the window at her palace grounds.

The woman was shaking in her chair, and tears had welled up in her eyes minutes ago. It had fallen to her to deliver the latest projections for the Barony

RIM Navy Academy program to the Baroness, and as expected, the numbers were God-awful.

As a part of the support of the Issians, and yes, the Master Adept too, the Baroness had committed to close their Navy Academy and instead send all their current, as well as future, candidates to Eons and the official RIM Navy Academy. It sure sounded simple and perhaps even not that expensive as it was imagined at the start. But in the past six months, those pie-in-the-sky plans had to be knocked together. Costs had to be established for the movement and housing of more than one thousand current Academy students over on Eons. Costs had to be established for their tuitions, their uniform allowances, and the insurance of the whole kit and caboodle of them too. There were collateral costs too, summer placements, and then midshipmen co-ops for each of the last two years of the full five-year program. Add to that the costs for the supply of three brand new frigates to be donated for the full ten years to the RIM Navy to be used as they saw fit—and one could see the costs were astronomical.

But as a part of the deal, broached by the Baroness herself to get the Master Adept to come over to support the Barony side in a recent RIM Confederacy issue, it was a done deal.

The Baroness came back from the window and

put a calming hand down on the shaking shoulder of the woman from accounting. "There, there ... um, Mindy, right?" she said and ignored the correction. "You'll just gather up those docs and then send them back to me in electronic format so that I can chip a few pennies off. Will you do that for the Barony, please, Mindy?" she said as she patted her shoulder again and then returned to her desk chair. Sitting, she waved the woman away and then said to her private office's AI, "Find me my aide," and sat back.

Moments later, that aide passed the woman from accounting who was just leaving, and she sat in the same chair and clicked on her wrist PDA once to record the session.

The Baroness thought for a second and then said, "Send the following off to Enki—EYES ONLY for our Captain Scott. Inform him of the following, please," she said and then held out a hand and counted with her fingers.

"One, that I hereby empower him to use whatever he needs to do to get me—well, correction, to get the Barony—the probe metal. Even on a shared basis, but we must be at least a part of the RIM syndicate that gets the metal for our use," she said. She nodded to herself, and *that was an easy one*, she thought.

"Two, that Captain Scott is also to use his

position, as the most senior Barony representative on that planet, to gain us whatever we can win from the ambassador's negotiations. This I realize will not be much, but if he can work his magic on Harmon, then so be it ..."

That she thought would allow him to stay as close to the negotiations as he could and perhaps even closer.

"And lastly, third, I suppose, I want Captain Scott to use his Adept Officer—Bram, I believe, to help him in any way that he might need to. Read those Enkians and read them well is what I'd suggest. Anything he needs, we'll—I'll—provide. Just have him ask," she said and that was it.

She looked at her aide and smiled just a bit. "Get that out, Mindy, and I mean STAT. And tell my sommelier I want to see him STAT too. I think some wine would be nice as it's lunch time somewhere," she said and walked back to the window.

Here, tucked in one of the central cores of the palace where she actually did spend her time, the windows pointed out to a large courtyard where the gardening was exquisite and an ongoing usual daily occurrence. Today, there were more than a dozen palace gardeners out there cutting, mowing, hoeing, raking, trimming, and pruning. The list was long and she watched for almost a whole minute before she was bored.

Now, where was that sommelier, she wondered as she tried to put those huge numbers out of her mind. *We really do need that probe metal to come to the Barony so that I can replenish our treasury ...*

It was supposed to be over lunch, but instead of meeting at one of the Officers' Mess cafeterias, Tanner had Bram come see him personally. They both left the bridge to go to the ready room that sat off to one side.

Tanner dragged up one of the extra chairs in the room and sat with his Adept Officer at the small round table in one corner. As the *Atlas* was passing over the Enkian planet in low orbit, at this particular moment, the ship was on the outer edge of that orbit, and while the planet filled part of the screen, there was nothing but black on the rest. As the UrPoPoian system lay at the very tip of the RIM, where the end of the arm was, there was only deep space, black as coal that stretched out for millions of lights. True, there were a couple of local system galaxies out there, and one was close enough it was a smudge of light no bigger than a cough drop, but they couldn't see it now. Instead, just the black of outer space—deep black they called it usually. *Nothing but empty outer space and perhaps dark matter,* Tanner thought, *but that was best left to astrophysicists, as we have other fish to fry.*

He gestured at the ice water in a big frosted glass pitcher he'd had his steward supply just a few minutes ago, and Bram nodded, his face still very sweaty from his trip just a bit ago across the sands of Enki. And of course, he'd had a fresh tea brought for him, and he took a sip.

He leaned forward. "Bram, give me the whole story—leave nothing out and hit all the points too," he said.

Bram nodded. "First, I checked—or rather had Lieutenant Irving check for me—the whereabouts of our stonecraw friendly. He is on a flight over to one of their Militia training camps—so he'd be out of the way."

"Smart thinking, Bram—dunno if I'd have thought about trying to find out where he'd be. And then?" Tanner said.

"Next, I walked very casually over to the Resources pyramid. I was ostensibly taking sand samples. I had a kit and stopped every few hundred feet to fill up one of those little bottles. Took me almost an hour and a half to walk that half mile or so, but eventually I got to their pyramid and entered through the grade-level access door.

"Again, smart thinking ..." Tanner, said and he meant it.

"Once inside, I inquired as to where there might be a public washroom, and I was directed to the unisex facility on that level. I pretended to get lost twice, in case they have interior security cameras, but we don't have any proof that might be true, do we?" he queried.

Tanner shook his head. "No idea really, but they have mentioned that they do not record court cases, so I'd doubt it," he said.

Bram went on. "So, I found the same stairs down and went all the way to the big door that leads into the food treatment center. Once there, I just entered, like I had business there, and from what I could see, there was only a single Enkian Resources techie there in the control station in the middle of the conveyor system. Not the one I knew, of course, a new one, and he just looked at me. I went right up to him, and by luck—didn't really consider this beforehand—he too spoke our English. I asked if the tech from yesterday was around and got the answer that I wanted—that his shift started in a half hour so I said fine, I'd just wait and that got a simple nod. So I stood off to one side as tray after tray of food pellets came up to the chem imprinting station. They entered and a few minutes later, the trays come out with their sprayed-on coating and then back down to the far end of the treatment center. But really, while I watched, I kept an eye on the area behind us where the full immersion of the feather coloring was to take place and saw that the seven caged racks were still standing on their respective pools, as yet un-done. It was an anxious half hour, but soon the Enkian I had met came in, and seeing me, he grinned right away and hustled his workmate out quickly."

Bram smiled and took a drink out of his plas-cup, before continuing. "Then, he asked me why I had come back, and I said to enjoy his first-ever food pellet immersion process and to congratulate him too. That seemed to work for him as he showed me on his console monitor the notes on what he was supposed to be doing—he did the translations as good as he could, I expect, and then it was time."

Tanner nodded.

"I reached inside his head and made him think that the button had been pushed and that the tanks were slowly sinking into their specialized tanks. Pretty easy, really, if I will offer that not only does an Enkian not react at all—but that they seem to really be quite malleable too. We watched those tanks sitting there, unmoving, and I made him think that they were totally immersed. We chatted about other stuff for those five minutes—did you know that Resources has only five mines that they use for ore extraction? I didn't have the time to drill down to find the probe metal mines, but with only five, it can't be that hard an investigation—sorry, I mean, for later," he said and slurped another big drink out of his glass.

"Then, I went back into his brain and showed him that the caged racks had risen back up and were standing there dripping all the excess liquid chems back down into their tanks. I held him there and made sure that we both commented that the racks were almost dry and ready for whatever was next. And that was it. We turned back and noted that the automatic conveyor had been processing the food trays just fine, and there were no flashing icons on the console monitor. No sign at all that a major event had been left out of the process. I wouldn't have written that AI like that, but the Enkians did."

Tanner nodded and poured Bram a big refill from the ice water pitcher.

It all looked like it had worked.

"Seems like we got away with this one. No mistakes and no way—unless it's recorded—for them to know. What happens now to these phony food pellets?" he said.

"Yes, I asked, thinking that it might be important too. At the end of his shift, my techie wheels each of those caged racks—they are all labeled by the way with huge colored muse icons—down to a special catering truck, I was told. Those folks take them to the Words Muse pyramid, and on graduation night, each of the graduating younglings eats just one and wakes up the next day with a fully colored feathered crest on their heads. At least that's what is supposed to happen—but not this time."

He smiled and leaned back. "And, if we understand how things work here—the one that will get the blame is the Words Muse leader—the Enkian in charge, Uigoeri Qor. Not the Resources section nor your techie either—but the man in the big chair. That should cause enough of an uproar that can, of course, be straightened out in a few days. But enough, we believe, to hurt the election chances of Qor to win the election to the position of head juror in a few days too. We got our mission done without anyone dying—and as you know, that's important to me. To the RIM too," he said.

"We're good to go, I think, Bram," he finished off and took a sip of his tea.

CHAPTER SEVEN

As the *Atlas* shuttle slowly set down on the landing pad, Tanner, Bram, and Kondo were all in shock—technology shock that was. They had left the city only a couple of hours back and had climbed up to go sub-orbital halfway around the planet. They came down near a huge spaceport tucked in an area near a set of mountains in the temperate zone of Enki.

Tanner saw more than three dozen rockets standing by their gantries, before he lost count. Older styled, solid fuel chemical rockets from technology more than a thousand years old stood there. Interspersed among them, they could see some liquid fuel trucks filling those rockets and cold-gas rockets along one side.

Against a long wall that was more than forty feet

tall were satellites of some kind on racks. The satellites were round with antennas projecting in various directions, some with what looked like primitive solar panels of some type, and there must have been a hundred of them. Next to them, a row of probes sat in cradles in groups of threes. Tanner noted they were the same dull red color as the one that had made it to Juno after almost sixty years in space, and that meant the red metal must be this mystery metal. That at least was interesting, Tanner thought, as they continued to stare at the visible equipment, the huge hangars, and various buildings.

"Sir, this stuff is, well, plain old, Sir," Kondo said as he shook his head.

"That might be, but it still gets the job done. The Enki are anything but technology buffs, XO," he said, and yet, he too was shaking his head.

Stonecraw Qew chimed in. "Please be aware that this is just one side of the whole port; we have much newer missiles and the like ahead, friends," he added, and all four of them smiled.

As the shuttle put down, Tanner thanked their pilot, Lieutenant Jenkins, and they disembarked as a group. Stonecraw Qew led the way, and they left the pad area and walked to a small bus. Onboard, the corporal said something in Enkian. Stonecraw Qew responded and they went down a small alley to a main throughway and got in line behind some trucks and a Jeep. As they went, Stonecraw Qew pointed out some of the various equipment depots and what the Resources or Militia sections used them for.

While riding the bus, Tanner thought about the probe metal, so he tried to steer the conversation in that direction but in such a way so as to not let the stonecraw know what he was angling for reconwise.

"StoneCraw, the pieces of equipment we see here are, well, totally functional. I mean, already made. Are they also manufactured here too?"

Stonecraw Qew shook his head. "No, Captain, not at all. All of the equipment is manufactured in various centers around Enki under the auspices of the Resources section, of course."

Tanner nodded but drilled down a bit. "For instance, where were those satellites built?" he asked.

"Over at Manufacturing Center Number Eight about, um, three hundred miles north of here. Shipped down as fresh builds, I think, twice a month, maybe three times, I really don't know for sure."

"And the probe-sized missiles, what about them," Tanner added.

"They come from much closer, I think, 'cause the

mines for that outer shell are mined just over there," he said as he pointed at the range of mountains not too far away on the horizon.

"The ores are mined, probe shells created right there in the foundry, and then the missile engines get their outer shells and then are shipped here. If we needed 'em daily, that could happen easy, but then how often do you need a probe?" he said.

Tanner, Kondo, and Bram all made a mental note of that and filed it away, but Tanner tried to push.

"If we're done here quickly, could we go and see the mines?" he asked politely.

Stonecraw Qew nodded. "We can do that, sure, my friends. But first, over here," he said as he pointed off to one side at some equipment and went on and on about those pieces.

Tanner let it go in one ear and out the other. In an hour and a half, Stonecraw Qew had finished his monologue. They'd moved hundreds of yards around the port and had seen just about everything one could imagine.

And now for the probe metal mines, Tanner thought as he broached the topic once more.

"Absolutely," Stonecraw Qew said as he led the way back to the bus, "and it's, as I said, pretty close too."

On the bus, the stonecraw regaled them with stories about how the spaceport had grown over the years and how new technology was always coming along. The three *Atlas* officers raised their eyebrows. *He really had no idea,* Tanner thought, *but that was fodder for another conversation.*

As the bus moved away from the spaceport, it took a lateral roadway that slowly veered off to the left. Miles later, those mountains were much closer and then almost upon them. The road once more veered to the left, and then directly ahead was a large group of buildings and trucks. There was also a huge berm of foundry supplies, like fuel or items needed for the forging of the probe metal from ore through to metal. Tanner had no idea what anything was, as his experience in mining was almost naught. He had little knowledge of foundry and the workings of it either. But he knew the basic process was that ore was heated, mixed with other items or supplies, and then poured out of a furnace to become metal once it cooled.

As the bus pulled up next to a building, Tanner noted one thing.

"Security? There is no gates or fences or for that matter, any way to keep people out, is there?" he asked.

"Why would we need security, Captain? All there is here is ore, and it's metal when it comes out of the foundry. Resources is usually the only people you'd ever see here—sorry, I've no idea then why security would be needed," he said, and Tanner could tell he was truly out to lunch when it came to a reason why it'd be needed.

At the door, Stonecraw Qew preceded them through and went down a long central corridor to a door near the end. Above the door hung a small sign that read, "MILITIA OFFICE." He turned to his left and went through the door. Inside, a few feet away, sat a Militia corporal at a desk. A bookcase and a couple of filing cabinets finished off the total furniture in the room.

"Sir," the corporal said as he quickly rose and gave the double-hand-to-chest salute.

"At ease, Corporal," Stonecraw Qew said, and he saw there were no chairs for his guests to be seated in.

He looked a bit upset but he nodded as the three RIM guests stood with him opposite the desk.

"Corporal, these are visitors from off-planet— you've heard that we are hosting a diplomatic team from the RIM Confederacy, no doubt?" he said.

The corporal nodded vigorously, which matched the sudden ripple in his feathered crest, and he clicked his beak once..

"Well, these are three of same—and we'd like to see the mines and a tour too, if possible?" he inquired.

"Sir, yes, Sir," the corporal replied, "and would

you like a tour guide too, Stonecraw?"

Stonecraw Qew nodded, and the corporal got on his console and made some quick keyboard strokes. The visitors in his office could hear the sound of footsteps running down the hall outside the office. A moment later, a breathless Resources Enkian, his black and lavender feathers all standing straight up on his head, entered the office and gave the traditional two-handed salute to Stonecraw Qew.

Introductions were made and Bram gave a "got it" hidden sign to Tanner to let him know that he could read the Enkian named Qal fine.

They moved off with guidance, turned to their left and went down the remaining hallway to a door in the back area. They went down the stairs and to their left again for a few hundred yards. At the entrance to what must be the mine, it seemed wrong in Tanner's mind, and he said so.

"Qal, I must ask, since this kind of a mine I've never seen before. Where is the major shaft down, the head-frame, the hoist buildings that are a normal part of shaft mining?" He'd seen just that kind of setup years ago when he'd been fighting the pirates on ITO, where the major industry had been underground hard rock mining, but he did not see any of that here and now.

"Ahhh ... yes, that is a long story, Captain, but here's the short form. We do not need to do shaft mining for the Xithricite metal—oh, that's the name of the find. About a billion years ago or so, a large asteroid plowed into Enki, it lies right ahead of us right here," he said as he pointed to the large mountain in front of them.

It looks nothing like an asteroid, Tanner thought.

"Of course, after a billion years or more, any shape that the asteroid did have would be weathered and acclimated to be a part of Enki, would that make sense?" Bram asked their guide.

"Exactly what we think too, Sir, and yet once we —well, wait, 'til we actually enter the asteroid, and you tell me," Qal said, as he continued to lead them toward a huge set of big metal doors that led inside the mountain. Those doors were at least four feet thick of solid reddish-colored metal—Xithricite they imagined—and the surprise was inside.

As they entered, they had to move out of the way of a large dump truck that had a full load of reddish-colored sticks, or grids, which looked anything but like a metal ore. They walked along the inside wall as the interior roadway turned slowly to the right. Farther and farther inside they went, and all around them, the scene was the same. The walls, floor, and ceiling looked like they were made out of some kind of a dark charcoal gray rock with variations in color and shade. Interspersed within that rock was red metal ore—but it didn't look like normal ore. Instead, it was a latticework of red sticks or twigs or fat wires about the thickness of Tanner's little finger. The grids were big but in no real pattern, just a cross hatching of the Xithricite metal.

They moved over to a deep inside wall, and staying out of the way of machines and Resources workers, they sidled up to the mined wall on the right. Tanner reached out and grabbed an edge of the red metal rod that was about at waist height and gave it a tug. It didn't move. He tried to bend it figuring that putting some friction into the rod would slowly weaken it, but it wouldn't even bend. He looked back at Qal and gave him a questioning look.

Qal nodded, pulled out a simple rasp from his back pockets, and handed it to Tanner, who used one edge to slowly saw through the Xithricite rod, and eventually, a piece came off. Returning the rasp file to Qal, he looked at the small finger-sized piece of Xithricite that lay in his hand.

"Do you have any idea why this ore is like this? I ask, Qal, as in my experience, ore does not usually take on this kind of a natural form."

And he meant that. While he'd not done a Gallipedia on that, he was pretty sure that metals did not come fully formed into this kind of a rod-like structure, and he made a mental note to check

Gallipedia later back on the *Atlas*.

Qal shook his head. "Sir, no, sir. This is just what we have for this Xithricite metal. It is so inexpensive to mine due to its ease of getting to it. We simply scoop it up using big automated cutting machines, put it into trucks, and deliver it a mile or so away to the foundry where it's melted in our furnaces and poured out as pure Xithricite metal into sheets. It's strong—about twice as strong as any other metal we have on Enki—cheap, quick turn-around from ore to final product too. So we do a lot of it. Course, the color is an issue. It will not accept any other color via using alloys, as any additives to the furnace settle out to be at the bottom of the ensuing product as its own layer. Nothing—well, nothing we have here on Enki—will alloy with Xithricite. So it's a single item alone. Oh, paint will stick, of course, but eventually the Xithricite kicks it off … seems like it has a mind of its own, Sir," he said and shrugged just as a human would have.

Tanner nodded and they slowly made their way back out of the mine, dodging trucks and crews as they did.

"How big," Kondo said, "is the size of the mine or asteroid?"

"We don't know really in that we don't know how deep it goes, but the area above ground here is approximately three miles long here by about two miles wide. Deepness is an unknown, but we have drilled down more than five miles, and we still get Xithricite coming up. Big? Yes, we suppose that it was a major climate changer, this asteroid's impact, but we know little more than that. However, there are some fossilized records from drillings in the south where back about that time, it seems that there were some major extinctions."

They all nodded. This kind of an impact with something this big would have caused some kind of life-changing events on any planet.

Qal walked them all the way back to the bus. "Stonecraw, can I call over to the foundry and arrange for a guide there as well?" he asked, trying to be a good Resources Enkian.

Stonecraw Qew looked at the three RIM visitors.

Tanner shook his head and said, "I suppose not, we do need to get back, but we thank you for your hospitality."

Everyone smiled and the visitors queued up to board the bus. Once on the bus, it turned around to leave the area.

"At least you got a souvenir," Stonecraw Qew said to Tanner..

Tanner nodded as he pulled the souvenir out of his pocket. It lay on his hand, a simple red-colored metal rod about three inches long. *This is the metal that this whole thing is all about,* Tanner thought as he replied to StoneCraw.

"Yes, it's a great reminder that Enki finds and uses what it needs on its planet. I've never heard of mining an asteroid before, but I now know it can be done—and done successfully too. Kudos to the Enki Resources section for that, Stonecraw," he said.

Stonecraw Qew smiled back at him. "Not at all, Captain. We do try to make use of our planet in the best ways possible. Might I ask for a favor, I believe it's called?"

Tanner nodded.

"Could I ask that we make haste on our way home? I've just had a message from my conda—the jurors want to talk to me STAT about this whole feathered crest color changing failure," he said.

Tanner nodded and as they entered the shuttle, he instructed Lieutenant Jenkins to get them back to the Enki capital city STAT, and the shuttle picked up quickly, spun, and then yawed, and they were aimed at being sub-orbital in moments.

Wonder what that's all about, Tanner thought, and he knew Bram was wondering too.

#####

Tanner sat between Ambassador Harmon and one of his aides in what he called the diplomatic VIP seats just two rows back from the edge of the

stage set in the middle of the huge rotunda in the
Words Muse pyramid. He was in his dress blues,
and his dang sidearm was sticking him in his ribs as
there was no room for it to drop down since the
seats were so jammed together. Many more seats
were there for all of the RIM members there too—
from the Caliphate, from the Duchy, from Faraway,
and from UrPoPo too. The vast numbers of
feathered heads present pulled his attention away
from the RIM members.

In fact, he thought, as he looked around in the
huge space, this was the most Enkians he'd seen
together since they'd arrived on the planet just last
month. There must have been at least a thousand
seats here on the rotunda floor add more seats in
the huge unfolded and erected bleachers that sat on
all four of the sides of the pyramid. They would
hold, as Tanner turned and scanned the wall-to-wall
Enkian faces that he could see, at least ten thousand
more. On the enlarged stage sat the younglings
who were attending their graduation ceremony,
and that'd be about four or five hundred more too.

"Quite a turnout, wouldn't you agree, Captain?"
Ambassador Harmon said as he glanced at the
crowds himself.

"Sir, yes, Sir," Tanner said and added "and the
temperature doesn't reflect that either. Wonder how
they cool such a huge space with so much body

heat." *I should ask someone about that, maybe Stonecraw Qew would know.*

Behind them, and Tanner had counted at least five rows, sat the few RIM Confederacy members who had showed up and worked their way into this big Enkian annual event. Each had gotten five seats, so the Caliphate sent five and the UrPoPoi had sent five too. With the forty or so on the real diplomatic mission to Enki, that made fifty RIM citizens seated to watch the ceremony.

They sat. They waited. Several minutes later, a parade of the leaders of all five of the muses entered in a single file, walking to a rather stirring music piece being played by the Music Muse players who were stationed along one side of the five-sided stage. Fine Arts Muse citizens were busy painting and sculpting the beginnings of the evening too. Dance Muse citizens had provided quite a colorful crew of what Tanner would call modern dancers, as it appeared to have no relation to tap or ballet or jazz. Tanner couldn't be considered a critic, but the dancers were pretty darn good. Words Muse citizens, as this was their own pyramid, had some simple desks setup and what looked like writers making journal entries, while Performance Muse citizens were doing some kind of a mime thing. On that, Tanner had no idea what much of it meant, but he could see this was the norm at such an event.

As the procession made it to the stage and up the stairs, the twenty-four of the leaders took their seats in front of each of their areas. The twenty-fifth leader, Uigoeri Qor, the leader of the Words Muse did not take a seat. *Our target,* Tanner thought, as the Enkian made his way to the front of the stage and took the microphone at the podium.

"I greet you all—and hereby open the six hundred and thirteenth graduation day ceremonies. Resources, please bring in the ceremonial presents," he said with great panache, and from off to one side, there was a stir.

As Tanner watched, along with the thousands of others, two Resources Enkians wheeled a caged food truck between them, and there were five of them in a row. Each wheeled their carts to the rear of the stage and then pushed them up to the stage. Each of the duos then moved the carts to stand in front of the rows of younglings beside the front row of the leaders of each muse.

As Qor watched, and was pleased, he smiled out at the crowds, his beak clicking a few times as his feathered red and white crest rippled over and over.

He is definitely in charge, and proud, and about to take a big fall, Tanner thought.

There were speeches by each of the five muse leaders, and each spoke at length about what a privilege it was for their muse to be growing by accepting these new younglings. Each muse leader spoke about the younglings who had excelled by having the best potential skill and ability to become a muse citizen. They glowingly talked about each of their muses, and each received a huge beak clicking when they were done.

Nothing could be more boring than hearing the same speech but with five different flavors in a row. But then again, I'm not an Enkian, so maybe I'm not the best critic, Tanner thought and smiled.

After the last muse leader spoke, Qor introduced a conda from the Militia who also spoke and reminded the whole enclave that they too were a part of Enkian life. The Militia provided safe, secure living for all Enkians, and being a Militia officer was a good position to aim at. Only a small part of the crowd responded, and the beak clicks were few and far between.

Following the Militia conda was a Resources speaker who nearly copied the same speech the previous speaker had used but reminded everyone present that it was the Resources section that did all the work on Enki to keep their world, society, and yes, muses up and running and fed and alive. *Good argument,* Tanner thought, *and most likely true too.*

Qor took back the podium and said as loud as he could, "Could we please have the Performance Muse younglings take center stage?" He moved off to one side.

More than a hundred younglings rose, formed an orderly single file, and then reformed in center stage into rows. As they did that, the five leaders of their muse-to-be took up the area directly in front of them and motioned for the food items to be brought up by the Resources duos. As they did, the Performance Muse leader, Eesuxo Qyn, gave the younglings their final instructions.

"You will repeat after me, younglings, to earn your new muse and new name, the name of Qyn," he said solemnly. As he made the salute sign of the Enki race, the younglings copied him.

Holding both hands heart high with the palms facing down, the younglings slapped them against their chests.

Qyn said in a slow and solemn tone. "We now accept the Performance Muse as our own personal muse and hereby swear to follow the statutes of the Enki race and hold only our muse as the true law of our lives. This we swear."

Each of said the younglings repeated Qyn's words as one of their new muse leaders passed among them putting a single food pellet directly into each of the youngling's open beaks.

Qyn smiled and dropped his salute, as did the younglings, and they all swallowed. Their white feathered crests, small as they were, made a final white ripple, and they all cheered, beaks clicking, and the thousands in the rotunda all clicked their own beaks.

It was a simple, but nice ceremony, and yet to Tanner, it was still a bit odd. But tomorrow he knew it'd be odder still to all of Enki.

He grunted when he realized that a major part of any diplomatic mission was the need to sit and be patient as the same things happened over and over and over. *Four more times of this same muse acceptance by the younglings.* Music Muse was next, followed by Dance Muse, then Fine Arts Muse, and finally the last muse, Words.

He paid a bit more attention to Qor of Words, as this was the final youngling graduation and Qor would be the one who would bear the responsibility for this evening's food laxity.

He smiled and nodded to the ambassador as the man made some comments about how lucky they were to attend such a normally private and highly personal event in Enki society. The ambassador droned on about how the younglings all looked so proud and how the muse leaders—especially Qor—had handled their chores with delicacy and skill.

Tanner nodded because that was what one did to an Ambassador, but he had his own take on that as he smiled and nodded once more.

223

Tomorrow, all hell is going to break loose, and that's for sure ...

#####

He lay on his big beautiful double-sized bed and stretched. He wondered what had awakened him. A moment later, there were three chimes, and he knew he had an incoming EYES ONLY and remembered he'd turned the volume dial down low.

Do I get up and look at it? Nope, too damn comfy.

"Room AI—who is on the other end of that incoming EYES ONLY?" he said. He realized that he probably should have added a please, but then when you talk to an AI, it's like talking to a toaster. And machines like an AI did not require manners. Still, his mom would have said ... and he shook off that whole side of him as the AI responded.

"Captain, it is the Lady St. August who is making this call—rather, it is coming from the *BN Sterling*, located on KappaD, it seems."

At least the AI was polite, he thought, as he quickly got up and padded over to his desk in his bare feet. Thinking about it for a minute, he went over to his bathroom, grabbed his emerald green robe to wear, and went back to his console right away. He smiled at his reflection in the monitor and quickly hit the proper button on his keyboard to connect with the caller.

Moments later, the Barony crest with its two crowns in blue and red appeared, held for a second or two, and then faded to black as the Lady's face appeared on the screen.

"Excuse me, Captain, for making such a call at this awful hour—I know that it's nighttime where you are, but I did want to speak to you," she said and then smiled widely. "That, and it is always nice to see you, Tanner," she said.

Tanner smiled. "Lady, what can I do for you— and it's always good to hear from you too, Helena," he responded, and they both grinned at each other.

She nodded, looked over to her left wherever she was, and then looked back at him after a few seconds.

"Captain," she said so he knew they were back to talking about Barony business, "I'm on KappaD and a guest here of the Alex'n hegemony local governor, which is neither here nor there. But what might be of interest to us—the Barony, I mean—is what happened here earlier today."

Tanner noted her voice had gotten somber. He wondered what could be going on with KappaD and quickly reviewed his knowledge of the planet. KappaD was one of the fifteen planets in the Alex'n realm at the southern border of the RIM beside the Pentyaan realm that lay outside of the RIM. The

Pentyaans, with more than twenty-three planets and systems in their realm, was the biggest and closest neighbor of the RIM Confederacy. They were asked every few years if they'd like to join and had always refused, hence the long-standing sanctions between the RIM and Pentyaan space. In fact, while the two sides were not at odds, they did have a mutual distrust and always were suspicious of each other.

"And what might have happened today, My Lady, that caused an issue?" he inquired.

She took a moment before she answered, and Tanner had no idea why she would need to measure her words.

"Today, a Pentyaan ship—a merchantman freighter of disreputable origins, I believe—showed up here on the fringe of the boundary between us and asked for refuge. Well, that was their word for what they wanted. According to them, they are seeking to 'escape from the tyranny of their Pentyaan masters,' and they have asked for us to provide them with 'refuge' by accepting them in as refugee immigrants to the RIM," she said, and her voice was still questioning.

He nodded but did not interrupt.

"The thing is, Captain, that no one has ever asked for 'refuge' here on the RIM —as far as I can tell at least, and that's both my own and the governor's memory at work here. Never before, so as far as we know, there is no precedent on what this means for us—or for them either. One thing, that my own Captain Flannery brought up, is the ship itself. People are one thing, but they want to also claim their ship and then sell it here on the RIM —to the RIM as a part of their navy they even said, to help finance their entry to our Confederacy. But as Flannery pointed out, the Pentyaans are going to be pretty upset with this to begin with—never mind losing an asset like a cruiser too. And in thinking about that, I'd have to agree," she finished off and looked at Tanner.

He nodded one more time and then took his time coming up with an answer. "Ma'am, for the RIM to accept refugees would be dependent upon our own statutes and laws, and I'm no lawyer. But that's as you said, people. But a cruiser is a whole other matter. Yes, I agree too with your captain—for the Pentyaans to accept losing a cruiser is most likely never going to happen. And that means that we'd be at odds with them, the RIM, I mean. This is a very interesting situation, Ma'am. Wish I was there. Oh, can you describe the Pentyaans, crew and all? Do they look like they need refuge?" He really had no idea, but he had in his past seen people who'd lost their homes and cities in war. They had not only that distant stare in their eyes, but they had an

entirely different way about them. He hadn't
known really how to handle the few he'd met, but
he did know that they just seemed lost and alone.

She nodded. "I've never in my whole life here on
the RIM met people who I consider more scared—
fearful, really. They all are very anxious, and they
look like they all suffer from a blanket set of fears—
but what about the Pentyaans could cause that, I've
no idea. While we know very little of them, they are
very much, I think, like us—well, as close as aliens
can be to we humans. The crew, their captain, their
techies, and their warrant officers—everyone I met
is like in slow motion with life as they are fearful of
what I don't know. But they are full of dread and
apprehension—that I know. And we've no idea
why other than the same thing they say over and
over—that they must find refuge from the
Pentyaans. A bit of a mystery, I think—which is
why I contacted you.

He tilted his head to one side and looked at her
questioningly. "Ma'am?" he said.

"I am hoping that you can get away from this
Enki diplomatic mission and get down here to
KappaD immediately so that you can help here. I
trust you're wider experience than anyone here has
and want you on this on behalf of the Barony. Can I
ask—can you get away from there now?" she asked.

He looked at her and realized he needed to be

honest with her. He took several minutes to spell out where the diplomatic talks were, why they were on hold, and what he and Bram had come up with regarding the graduation and food pellets. He explained how they believed that would fix the election next week to swing to the Fine Arts Muse and ensure that the RIM diplomatic offer would be accepted. And, he noted, the probe metal would come to the RIM too.

She listened. She nodded. She asked a couple of questions—including what they'd do if the election did not go as planned for which he had no answer at all yet. She nodded again and then spoke.

"Fine, then you can't leave just yet. You need to stay until the deal is a done one—say sometime next week right after the election—but then I want you down here on KappaD STAT. Use the *Atlas* like she was made, and get here as soon as you can. Do we concur?" she said.

Tanner nodded and they smiled at each other.

"Ma'am, one thing? In my experience, refugees always are scared and afraid but never of where they've just come from. Instead, they are scared of where they are going as well as their acceptance there. So if you think that the fear is from something behind them, that's just bloody odd, Ma'am. You be careful, yes, and keep a couple of those blue-booted EliteGuards close, Ma'am. Yes?"

he asked, and she nodded back to him too.

The EYES ONLY ended quickly, and he sat alone for a moment, wondering if he'd be able to get back to sleep at this point and noted that his alarm would be going off in less than two hours. "Might as well stay up," he said to himself, and that meant the gym.

He slipped off his robe and went to find workout clothes. *Damn*, he thought, *no clean shorts*. He grabbed the cleanest pair he could find in his dirty laundry bag and slipped them on. *Hell with it*, he thought, *who else is gonna be there at this time of the night?*

He left his quarters up on Deck Five, went down the stairs to Deck Nine, and then back toward the officers' gym. As he went through, the AI chimed at him, and he said, "What's up, AI?"

AI replied quickly and asked if he would like to update his registry and add in today's workout to his totals and he agreed.

When he went down the long main aisle to the rows of treadmills, he was surprised to see one other soul there already—Kondo, his XO.

"Should'a known," Tanner said to himself as he took the machine beside his XO and quickly got up and into stride as the AI took care of all the settings and paces. He worked hard, telling AI to up the pace twice while his body slowly got back into the swing of working out.

I really hate this. It's stupid to have to exercise. Anyways, why is there no pill for that?

He worked harder then, and AI responded with another pace change. His breath began to get labored and thick. The sweat poured off his brow, and he shook his head every few minutes to try to get the sweat off his forehead and his eyebrows. He worked hard. His body worked hard, but he knew that he was getting on—forty in less than a month was the mantra he didn't want to think about.

Kondo finished before him and moved off his treadmill to sit on a bench off to one side to wait for him.

Instead of just stopping, Tanner ran his full twenty minutes, and then the AI turned off the machine. His breathing very harsh and thick, he went over to sit beside his XO.

As his breathing slowed and he drank a big bottle of water to re-hydrate, Kondo just sat and rested himself.

Eventually, he got his wind back, and he half-turned to talk to him.

"Damn body is getting older, XO," he said with a half-grin, which got him a nod of agreement.

They passed the first few minutes commiserating about exercise, their bodies, and why there was no pill yet.

After that, they talked about their current situation here on Enki—about the upcoming failure of the food pellets and that it should happen today. Kondo admitted he was up early because of that alone.

Tanner started to admit to that too, but then he shook his head, told Kondo about the new Pentyaan refugee situation, and asked for his counsel on that too.

Kondo thought quietly for a moment and said he could add little. In his experience on Amasis, he offered that everyone who got there claimed either some kind of refugee status to gain immigrant status or they arrived rich and didn't need to apply at all as entrepreneurs. Other than that, he offered, he knew little. But when questioned, he agreed with Tanner that all refugees feared what lay ahead—not behind.

Both sat and cooled off even more, and Tanner groaned as he rose on his tired legs and grinned again at his XO.

"Thanks for the counsel, Kondo. Later—see you on the bridge in about an hour or so," Tanner said.

Eecesoe Qig, leader of the Fine Arts Muse, turned and looked out the bright blue windows at the circle of pyramids that surrounded the

Resources pyramid in the center of the capital city of Enki. He knew he had to come up with a response, but what it would be he had no idea yet, so he turned back to the Caliphate captain who sat opposite him.

"Captain Abu al-Hasan, yes, I do understand what the thrust of your asked-for meeting is today. But I still have a problem trying to understand the difference between the RIM offer from the ambassador and your own from the Caliphate."

Qig smiled and to anyone who might have been watching, he looked like he was being honest. But in fact, he not only fully understood, he was playing a negotiating card to see what the eager alien across the table might give up.

The captain nodded and looked down at his tablet, but he wasn't reading it at all; instead, he was trying to judge how far to go if he was to sweeten his offer.

"Leader Qig, there are really some major differences—especially when one considers that becoming a full voting member in the RIM Confederacy is such a costly enterprise," he said as he scrolled the page on his tablet to read out the short list.

"One, you will become a full member which means that you will share one fortieth or so of the costs of the operation of the joint ventures of the

RIM and its various bodies and departments. You will be tithed with your share of everything from the RIM Navy to our marines, air force, and all of our resource needs too.

"Two, you will be tithed with your share of the costs of full government departments that are used to run the RIM. That would include our Health and Safety, Customs, Excise, and Tax departments. Our judiciary and our Provost guards as well. Our full seven shipbuilding centers spread around the RIM. Our shares of the higher education facilities too, like the Navy Academy on Eons, the Air Force Academy on the planet Ttseen, and the marines over on Combat in the Duchy. There are a ton of costs of same, and each and every single member of the Confederacy gets their share of costs to pay for as well," he said as he continued to look down at his tablet.

Qig nodded thinking perhaps of what kind of costs those items would add up to in a year.

"Three," Captain al-Hasan said, "you will be required to attend our RIM Confederacy Council meetings, on a monthly basis. Each and every month, you'll be sent an Agenda for your knowledge of upcoming issues, discussions, and final voting on same. You need to be on Juno every month, which may be an issue for you, I'd believe.

"And lastly, four, we here in the RIM

Confederacy believe in the simple fact that united we stand. We face every single threat, incursion into our Confederacy as a united front—no matter the cost in credits or in lives. It's what makes us strong out here on the RIM," he finished off his short list.

Qig nodded one more time. "And how, as that is what we're already offered by the RIM ambassador, is that any different than your own offer—the Caliphate's offer, I should say?"

Captain al-Hasan nodded back and held out his hands, palms up, as if to show that he was being open and honestly frank.

"Leader Qig—we, the Caliphate, offer the option of Enki, under your leadership as the new head juror, to become one of the members of our own realm, the Caliphate. As I've already said, that would mean that not a single cost that I just listed would be an Enkian item. Those costs—all of those costs—would be paid by the Caliphate itself. Enki would become a full member of the Caliphate realm, would attend the RIM Council meetings, and sit with the rest of the members of the realm too," he said and smiled.

Qig chose that moment to go all in. "And to do that—to get to Juno on a monthly basis—will the Caliphate give us FTL technology for us to be that full member of the Caliphate?"

Captain al-Hasan had no inkling this was

coming, but he really wasn't surprised. The big technology that was missing from Enki was faster than light speed for their ships. Without it, they'd never be any kind of a member — the captain knew that would be true.

"Yes, I have been enabled to offer up first, a pair of frigates that yes, have FTL as their basic technology. You can use them as you see fit, of course, as full members of the Caliphate. As well, we will accept in our Engineering Academy your own Resources technicians, who will be trained and taught — at no cost to Enki — on how to build and maintain the FTL technology too. Again, this is our best and final offer ..."

Qig nodded. His "all in" had worked as he could simply say yes and then he'd have acquired FTL technology for Enki — at no cost at all.

He wondered, though, if that really was the captain's final offer.

On the *Atlas* bridge, Lieutenant Irving was getting quite a workout as she answered Ansible calls, messages from Enkians, and EYES ONLY from Ambassador Harmon direct through to her captain. Tanner thought she looked like one of those octopi from DenKoss, with the ten arms that could reach out in their own direction. Her hands were flying on the Ansible console connecting, disconnecting, and putting conference calls into effect. "Amazing what a glitch in the Enkian society could cause," he said to himself, as he quickly wiped the smile off his face and nodded to his Ansible officer that he'd take the ambassador's fifth call of the morning.

All the Ansible calls had to do with the same thing. This morning, all over the five muse pyramids, not a single youngling had arisen with colored feather crests. All stayed white—and that made all the muse citizens see red! So far, the Militia, the RIM group had found out, had quelled two brawls when upset citizens had gained entry into the Words Muse pyramid and had gone on trashing sprees. The display on one wall of the pyramid rotunda had been spray-painted, and the documents, some of which were old and valuable— or had been before—had been destroyed.

The Dance Muse leaders had gathered together all of their new citizens and had marched their younglings over to the Words Muse pyramid in protest. They gained entrance somehow, even though the Militia had cordoned off the whole Words Muse pyramid, and the Dance Muse leaders had gotten those younglings chanting that they had been cheated by the Words Muse and they wanted justice.

Ambassador Harmon skipped a greeting and updated Tanner on the current situation. "Captain, there appears to be some kind of a group of Music Muse Enkians who are marching on the Words Muse pyramid, and while they're speaking Enkian and not English, I'm told they're looking for blood. Qor's blood, they say, as it was his doing that the feathers did not turn," he said.

Tanner nodded and took a moment before he answered.

Ambassador Harmon was nervous, no doubt about that, Tanner thought. He also was worried about what would happen—this was without precedent here on Enki. This had never happened before, and no one knew what it meant—what it did to the status of the newly graduated younglings. Were each of the muses allowed to accept their new graduates without the color change? Currently, no one could tell which of these new graduates were members of which muse. No identifying feathered crest meant that these new graduates were not full muse citizens.

The ambassador shook his head. "Captain Scott, I'll keep you in this loop, but at this point, I still feel very safe here in the Words Muse pyramid. As you know, our on-site quarters are up three floors off the main grade rotunda level, and we are fully protected by a full platoon of RIM marines. And yes, thank you for sending down the extra platoon of EliteGuards too, we are fine, I believe. It's Qor and his leaders that I think might be at risk—at least today. Most likely, as in all things, this will settle down tomorrow. Of course, there are considerations to be made about the election next week, but then I'm sure that Qor has that in mind as well. We all just wonder what happened to this food pellet situation is all ..." He nodded to Tanner and then disconnected.

Guess being a diplomat meant you can just quit a conversation anytime, Tanner thought. *Soon enough. Soon enough, this would all come to a head ...*

CHAPTER EIGHT

Iavoesi Qax, head juror, stood, and his crest rippled, but it did little in the current circumstances. Normally when he stood and the crowd noticed, they instantly quieted and all took their seats and the whole rotunda seating was silent.

Not today.

Instead, there were still hundreds of citizens of all the muses talking, arguing, yelling, and almost coming to blows. This time in the Words Muse pyramid, all five of the muses were represented by their citizens. Each of them had their younglings, the recent graduates from the big ceremony just two days ago, seated in the front of each of their bleachers. All, Tanner could see, still had the white feathers of a youngling.

On the stage were the leaders of each of the five

muses, as well as the jurors. And Qax, realizing he was not going to be able to use his position to gain silence, called over a Militia officer. Moments later, a huge siren sounded. The wailing siren filled the rotunda and got everyone's attention. Most of them sat down quickly.

"I must apologize to one and all for my use of the storm siren, but it comes to me that this is very apropos. We are facing a storm—unexpected, huge, and yes, perhaps even changing our way of life here on Enki. Please, take your seats—we have a statement to make ... please be seated," he said over and over.

Eventually, the thousands in the rotunda area were seated. They were quieter than before, but the grumbling from the muse citizens was still loud. Tanner waited to hear what Qax would say about the younglings and their feathers that had remained white. He sat in the small seating area that had been provided for the RIM diplomatic team. As well, the Caliphate was there, the captain of the *Pollux* and a few of his officers were there too, tall in their seats as they always were. A few more RIM members from UrPoPo were also present, but that was about it this morning as the emergency meeting had just been called.

Ambassador Harmon sat right up front, but Tanner had been lucky enough to duck out of that row and move to the back one to sit beside Bram.

"We okay, you think?" he asked Bram, hiding his mouth behind a hand over his face.

"Should be. I can see nothing to be worried about at this juncture," Bram said as he looked around and then looked at Tanner. "About twenty feet is the limit—I lose them when they get farther away than that," he said, and Tanner knew his unasked question had been answered.

On stage, Qax moved to one side to confer with the same Militia officer, and moments later, a company of Militia soldiers took up picket duty around the stage with three platoons per side. Tanner and the thousands of muse citizens noticed, and that deployment started some whispered conversations going, but Qax ignored that and went back to the podium.

"As the rest of you, I too am surprised that the current graduating class of younglings have all failed to change their crests; not a single feather has changed to its proper muse colorations. We all know that this has never happened before. And yes, there could be many items to consider—"

Some Enkian from the Fine Arts Muse seating bleachers yelled out, "The Words Muse is responsible, they ran the event," which started catcalls, yelling, and beak clicking about the Words Muse and the Resources section too.

"And yes, thank you for that—the event was run by our Words Muse, and I think the event was a success. And as someone else has also added, our Resources section is in charge of the food treatments too. We will be beginning our investigations into how this happened so that we can prevent it from ever happening again. Of course, that may lead to someone who has done this for a reason that as yet, we do not know ..."

That got a huge response from the crowd, as there were many callouts and more beak clicking.

"We will investigate. We will determine what happened and how and then work on the changes needed to prevent this from ever happening again. You have my word on this—the whole jurors' words, in fact," he said, and that got him a rousing roar from the crowd.

Tanner knew, of course, what had happened. He also knew that as he and Bram had planned, some in the crowds today put the blame squarely on the Words Muse as being the responsible party. He also knew that the Fine Arts Muse would be talking that position up all over the city in the next few days up until the election.

"This should work, right," he thought to Bram, and Bram gave him a thumbs-up signal.

"One final thing," Qax said as the emergency meeting was coming to a close, "we will be

supplying each of the five muses with new food
pellets that we know will work as expected. So
sorry for this, one and all—but we will get to the
bottom of this disaster very, very soon." His
feathered crest rippled one more time. Beaks
clicked in unison all over the rotunda as the crowds
were happy with the proceedings.

So far, we all are, Tanner thought, *so far ...*

#####

"All right, Captain—what the hell is going on?
I've been held up for over three hours with the
jurors in their investigation, and it's obvious that
they are looking at us—the RIM diplomatic team—
as having something to do with this whole feather
change issue. Since things have cooled down a fair
bit, we've sent back our extra EliteGuard platoons
and kept only the one squad of Provost Guards.
The Enkians we see and meet are all grumbling
under their breath but don't seem to be doing any
sort of rioting or the like. We like that, of course.
And the re-treatment of new food pellets has been
successful, as the younglings now all have their
feathered crests changed to their proper colorations.
Still touchy though, we see, and that's annoying to
say the least."

He half-smiled at Tanner before continuing. "We
have been busy though as I've been asked to sit in

on a host of interviewees, everyone from the leader of all five muses, both Militia and Resources sections, food handlers from manufacturers through to the Enkian who applied the chemical treatments, to truck drivers, caterers, and just about all of the Words Muse pyramid workers too. But what I want to know is—did we play any part in this?"

Ambassador Harmon was agitated, and as Tanner stood in front of his desk, he had only a few seconds to consider what to tell the man. He knew the office, as their Provost guards checked it daily, was un-bugged and clean. So anything he said would be for the ambassador only; the Enkians would never know.

Harmon must have been thinking the same thing as he said, "Room's clear, Captain, or so the Provost team said this morning. We borrow the offices, yes, from the Words Muse group, but we were told it was ours and would be kept that way."

Tanner nodded and then explained exactly what had happened in the past few weeks. He started with the threats from the Fine Arts Muse and their leader, Qig, who wanted the head juror position in tomorrow's election. He shared that he had made a deal, but he knew it would require he somehow keep the election's favored son, Uigoeri Qor, the head of the Words Muse, from winning. He also had known, he told the ambassador, that the best way to do that would have meant murder, and he couldn't do that. Tanner gave the ambassador the details of a plan he had hashed out with Bram, after more tours of the Resources had offered up a way to perhaps win that election for the Fine Arts Muse. They—well, Bram actually, as he could control Enkians quite easily—would simply fake the processing treatment of the big first dose of the chemicals that change Enkian feathers. The fault would lie wherever, but as the Words Muse was in charge, it meant that Qor would wear the issue like a badge of disappointment. Hence, they hoped that Qig would win the head juror's position, and that would mean the diplomatic mission would be successful. Enki would become a member of the RIM Confederacy, and the Xithricite metal would be available.

As he said that last bit, he leaned forward and placed that short Xithricite metal rod from the trip to the asteroid mine just yesterday on the ambassador's desk,.

Harmon leaned back, then forward to pick up the metal rod, and then back again. He stared at Tanner, then off into space for a moment, and then back at his captain.

"You've never considered a role in the diplomatic corps, have you, Captain? Because if you ever do, I'd be pleased to help you get a leg up immediately," he said, and he smiled at Tanner and then went on.

"You seemed to have found a way to circumvent —very nicely, I might add—the whole issue of getting rid of an election candidate. Bram was obviously successful; I hear nothing but grumbling about Words Muse all over the city, which should be reflected tomorrow during the election, and lastly, if it does not work, then we can simply claim later that Fine Arts Muse is at fault. At least we can try before they launch those cases against Words Muse," he said.

Tanner nodded. He hadn't thought that idea would have any merit, but one never knew.

"So, was I wrong in not taking you into my confidence, Ambassador?" he asked, his voice soft.

"Not at all, Captain. I fully believe in the strategy of 'need to know,' and I didn't need to then. Now, I'm aware and perhaps able to help too, if needs be. So far, though, all of this is hush-hush—classified, in fact. Who knows, Captain—the full list, please?"

Tanner nodded and had only three names, his, Bram's, and Kondo's.

Harmon nodded. "Few, that's good. And I trust as you're all crewmembers, you can count on their secrecy on this matter too. Am I correct, Captain?"

Tanner nodded.

"Good, so we're going to sit back and do nothing,

agreed Captain?" he asked.

Tanner nodded, but he had one question. "Ambassador, you mentioned that there had been quite a long list of interviewees—is there a list?" he asked.

Harmon nodded and reached into one of his "In" Baskets on his desk, riffled through the pile, found the list, and then handed it to Tanner.

Tanner thanked him and took a quick scan. Yes, there was the name of Resources Officer Swanki, actual Enkian who Bram had made make the mistake on the food. So that meant that he had been interviewed. That meant that if there was no AI recording—and they had that knowledge that this was true—then the jurors would believe the chemical treatments had been done as ordered. So they'd move on and look to see if the treated foods were somehow substituted with untreated pellets. They'd follow the trail away from the actual point of origin, which was natural and would lead to no guilty parties. Tanner smiled to himself.

"Sir," Tanner said, "I should have keyed you into this a bit earlier—but it only happened last week, but that's not an excuse. While diplomacy is not my thing, this has been quite an experience, Ambassador," he said and saluted, spun on his heels, and then left the RIM offices.

#####

In the huge rotunda of the Words Muse pyramid, the election headquarters for the new leader of the jurors was being held. There were huge screens dropped down from above, showing returns from all over the capital city, all with the names of each of the candidates and their current vote totals. Every so often, one of the media services would appear on screen with an interview, an exit poll, or an issue out in the city with polling stations and the like. With only six candidates, interviews with the candidates weren't an issue as someone always wanted to say something.

"Polls close when, Lieutenant?" Tanner asked Lieutenant Irving, his Ansible officer on the bridge. She looked down at her console and said, "In about an hour, Sir," and she made some clicks on her keyboard.

On the huge view-screen on the bridge, the whole of the rotunda shifted as Irving moved the camera's point of view on the drone they were running in the space well above the crowds below. They were also providing the feed from their drone to the UrPoPo ship, the Caliphate ship, the Faraway ship, and via Ansible back to Juno too. *Don't know,* Tanner thought, *if anyone is even watching back there, but the feed is going out for sure.* The sidebar listed the feed as being up, streaming, and live. Further, he noted, the stage had been populated already with the other four jurors who were not leaving their positions. There were a few others there as well along with the leaders of each of the five muses. As Qig of Fine Arts Muse and Qor of Words Muse were both candidates, they were present but not very sociable at all. *Didn't matter,* Tanner thought, *that one of them was probably the winner.* He'd charged his Science officer, Lieutenant Commander Karl Sheldon, with the job of getting some kind of projections together for the election. He'd worked at it diligently and had put the report on his captain's desk just this morning. Two of the candidates ran every time; they were always also-rans, and they had no chance of even placing let alone winning. Then there were the two current leaders of Words Muse and Fine Arts Muse who were the front-runners. The final two candidates were outsiders, never having even been in the leadership of a muse, and they were the two dark horses in this election. Both were members of the Dance Muse, and both were the exact same as the other—they had come from what they pushed as a bonus for their fans, a twin-yolk egg. Twins, Tanner called them. They looked alike —of course, all Enkians looked very similar—but these two were like mirror images. Both tended to do a little swing step when they talked, but that was normal for Dance Muse citizens. *Dark horses, indeed,*

Tanner thought. But the big two were Qig versus Qor—and he knew that was where the play would come from.

Ambassador Harmon, along with all of his diplomatic team, entered the rotunda led by some Words Muse pyramid workers, and they took their seats off to one side of the main stage. Filling up the bleachers were Enkians who Tanner figured had probably already voted, and they sat anywhere as no sections had been reserved up front. As he watched, some formed little cells of conversation, talking, laughing, arguing, and generally being social. Others sat quietly, somehow alone among thousands, and yet watching everything with an eagle eye.

"Polls close in ten minutes," a voice said over the whole rotunda.

Automatic polling AI, it appeared, looked after the polls themselves, but Tanner wasn't really sure. Automation didn't really exist on Enki, at least to a level that he was both familiar and comfortable with at this point. *Ten minutes 'til we find out whether or not our subterfuge worked*, he thought, and as he looked to his right to Bram, sitting in the bridge Adept Officer chair, he got a nod back. He glanced at the view-screen again and told his Ansible officer to ensure she got coverage of whatever was happening on the stage and to feed the content from the huge screen in the rotunda to their sidebar display as well.

Moments later, there was an announcement that the polls had just closed and tabulations would now ensue, followed by a triple chime of bells.

Wonder how long that'll take, he thought, and just as he thought that, the *Atlas* sidebar showed some returns.

With only seventeen percent of polls reporting, the Fine Arts Muse leader, Eecesoe Qig, had taken a small lead over the Words Muse leader, Uigoeri Qor, with the twins holding up similar numbers in spots three and four. The other two were coming up behind — way behind. Some media outlet ran a quick exit poll interview, and Enkians commented that yes, they had changed their mind as a result of the feathered crest incident, while others hadn't even heard about it.

Nothing like a population of voters who had no clue as to what was going on around them.

A triple chime rang once again with the update that forty-nine percent of polls were now reporting. The Words Muse leader, Qor, had taken a small lead, and that was unexpected. "Then again, playing the odds of their subterfuge had been a risk," Tanner said to himself.

He looked at Bram and grimaced but said nothing.

Again, there was a feed from a media source over in the Dance Muse pyramid where the twin candidates were being interviewed together. Neither, Tanner noted, had much to say other than they were really counting on the later returns, as one of them for sure was going to be the next leader of the jurors.

Confidence was a needed trait in any leader, Tanner knew, but these two were both in a world of their own.

Three more chimes sounded, and now with eighty-one percent of polls reporting, Resources was now able to make a projection on the winner—and it was going to be Eecesoe Qig of the Fine Arts Muse, and down in the Words Muse pyramid, the crowds were now all up and cheering or booing but involved somehow.

"It worked," Tanner said to himself, and he held up a clenched fist and noted that beside him Bram did the same, and he turned back over his right shoulder and yes, Kondo too. Mission accomplished. *No need to cheer*, Tanner thought, but he felt good about the hard work and personal involvement of Bram in getting this all done and would not forget that.

Maybe once we're back in the Barony, I'll find a way to show my appreciation ...

#####

"Sir, I've got Ambassador Harmon on his secure PDA—EYES ONLY for you, Sir," Lieutenant Irving said, and then she glanced down at her console which began to flash at her again.

"And, Sir, we have a force—more than fifty Militia soldiers being held down in the landing bay. Seems they came up with no advance notice nor for that matter request to dock—they say, Sir, that they are serving an arrest warrant on Lieutenant Bram Sander, Sir."

Tanner just looked at her, not fully understanding what she was saying, and he shook his head and said, "Say again, Lieutenant?"

"Sir, there are more than fifty Militia fully armed soldiers being held in the landing bay with an arrest warrant for Lieutenant Sander. Our own marines have them at gunpoint, Sir, but they say they're not going anywhere without him, Sir," she said and then clicked a few buttons on her console, and the rotunda of the Words Muse pyramid disappeared and the landing bay down on Deck Five on the *Atlas* came on screen.

A shuttle, quite a bit bigger than what he'd have thought the Enkian Militia might have, sat a distance away from the AI camera. In between its POV and the shuttle stood the fifty Militia fully armed soldiers. Each had an assault rifle in their hands, pointed down but still ready to use, and each was dressed in full flak suit armor. A couple of Militia officers stood in front of the troops spread out to form a major front. One, Tanner could see, was a conda—the Enkian equivalent of a general. Beside him were a couple of colonels and a stonecraw.

Opposite them, seen only from their backs, stood a hundred or so *Atlas* marines in full combat gear, their own assault rifles and sub-machine arms pointed directly at the opposing Militia soldiers. Standing at the rear was the *Atlas* marine colonel who was duty officer of the day, Anderson, Tanner thought, but he couldn't see the man's face clearly.

"Lieutenant, notify the duty officer down there that I'm on my way—have him tell that to the conda there, please. Transfer the ambassador's call to my PDA—authorization code C-A-P-6-6-H-N. Have a full company of marines put opposite the landing bay on the other side—have them come up the internal stairwell and stay in same but as close as possible to the bay, and put them under the control of the duty officer—and notify him. Bram, Kondo, you're with me," he said, and he stood and quickly moved out of the bridge, turned to his right, and started to trot down Deck Five toward the landing bay more than a thousand feet away.

As he trotted, he clicked his PDA and got the

ambassador who had left him a message after holding for what must have been too long for an ambassador. Simple message—the Militia was under orders from the jurors to come and arrest Lieutenant Sander as they had proof that he was responsible for the feathered crest color fiasco. Armed militia, Harmon said, with orders to take Sander in under an arrest warrant for trial here on Enki. Forewarned was forearmed but remember the rule of law, Harmon had finished off. That got a hint of a smile out of Tanner as he continued to trot, Bram and Kondo just a few steps behind him. It did take a bit to travel those thousand feet, and they were not impeded as every single crewmember moved out of their way in an instant. *Guess they don't see bridge officers running down the main deck too often.*

A few feet ahead, Tanner slowed and then stopped. Under the circumstances, while he was the captain of the *Atlas*, he already had a colonel in charge of the situation within the landing bay, and he knew he'd have to be a bit mannerly when he entered. He made his way to and then through the outer doorway off to the right of the corridor and into the landing bay.

It was as he'd already seen—two forces, opposed to each other, arms drawn and yet frozen. Between them stood his colonel, and on the other side, the

256

Enkian conda and his retinue stood. All frozen. All waiting for him.

This must go well, he thought.

He walked slowly but solidly around the backs of the ranks of his own marines to the open space far off to the right-hand side of the big landing bay. He turned to his left and made his way, keeping his eyes on the eyes of the conda, who half-turned to watch him, as he moved directly to the side of his own colonel.

"Colonel Anderson, I see we have visitors here on the *Atlas*," he said calmly and politely.

Anderson half-turned to face his captain and just nodded.

"And as yet have our guests made their wants known to us?" he asked politely, which got him a simple "no, Sir," from the colonel.

Nodding, Tanner stepped forward, faced the Militia force directly, and said quite clearly and politely, "Conda, I am Captain Tanner Scott of the *Atlas*. What can we do for you today?"

The conda was a bit surprised, he thought, as the conda held out his hand and one of his colonels beside him handed him a document. The conda looked down at it for a second to confirm that it was the proper item, and then he held it out to Tanner.

"Captain Scott, I'm Conda Yabesui Qem, sent to your ship with this arrest warrant for one

Lieutenant Sander, under orders from the jurors of Enki. We are under orders to do just that, Captain," he said, as Tanner took the single sheet of paper out of his hand.

He looked down at it, realized it was in Enkian, so he couldn't even read it, and looked up at the conda. "Conda Qem—are you here to serve this warrant upon Lieutenant Sander?" he asked.

Conda Qem nodded and replied, "Yes, Captain."

Tanner stared at him and wondered what might happen should he refuse to honor this warrant. There'd be combat right here in the landing bay, and then the whole RIM diplomatic mission would be canceled. They could go and not miss Enki—but then again, there was the damn Xithricite metal issue to think about too. As he stood there pondering that, Bram walked right by him and faced the conda himself.

"Conda Qem, I am Lieutenant Bram Sander and I submit to your warrant—you may take me into custody, Sir," he said, and there was a gasp somewhere behind Tanner.

As Bram held out his hands to be cuffed, Tanner stepped forward to stand beside his lieutenant.

"Conda—I would expect that you will be transporting my officer down to the capital city, where he will be put into custody in the Militia pyramid. Do I have that correct?" he asked.

"You do, Sir," the conda said as one of his colonels slapped cuffs onto Bram's wrists and then took his upper arm and stood rock still.

Still might go any way at all, Tanner thought.

"Sir, I'll be fine in the Militia custody. Come see me tomorrow, please, and then let's get to the bottom of this whole mistake. Colonel, let's go," he said.

They slowly moved through the ranks of the Militia soldiers behind them, toward the Enkian shuttle. Moments later, they stepped up the landing ramp and went inside.

Tanner looked at the conda in front of him. He didn't bother shaking a finger in the Enkian's face, but his tone said it. "Conda Qem—I wanted to go on record. You are charged with the duty of care and control of our officer. No harm, not a single thing, is to happen to our lieutenant. You have the duty to provide just that—you and all of Enki whom we also will hold responsible. Do you understand me, Conda?" he said, and there was no way anyone could have misunderstood.

The conda nodded and saluted, which Tanner replied to in kind.

Battle lines drawn, Tanner thought and turned to his colonel as the last of the Enki Militia soldiers finally got on their shuttle and the doors closed.

#####

"I have called this meeting to discuss what the current status of Lieutenant Sander is—and what our plans will be at his trial, which I've just been told will begin tomorrow. Captain?" Ambassador Harmon said, picking up his tablet and holding it so he could make notes.

Like there will be any, Tanner thought, as he looked around at all the people present in the conference room on the *Atlas*. Members of the diplomatic team were there: a representative from the Duchy ship, the *DN Triumph*; another from the Caliphate ship, the *CN Roc*; one from the UrPoPo ship, the *UN Andiya*; and another from the Faraway ship, the *FN Kamloops*. All were seated at the table including Tanner and Kondo from the *Atlas*. Twelve members from the RIM would plan Bram's defense. All had a voice today, but Tanner knew that the major spokesperson at the table was the ambassador. *And me,* which he felt was even more true.

"Cards on the table, Ambassador?" Tanner queried first.

The ambassador nodded back as permission to speak freely in front of all in the room.

It took quite a bit of time to explain what the background of the current situation was, but he spared not a single item.

He talked first about the value to the RIM

260

Confederacy of the probe metal—Xithricite as it was called here on Enki and how it was the most important major consideration of all. All other things were in third place, he said—except that now Bram had been arrested by the Militia here on Enki.

He went on to show the assembled defense team about the pressure that he and the ambassador had received from the Fine Arts Muse leader, Eecesoe Qig, and how they had threatened to halt the diplomatic talks no matter how they were going by filing case after case with the jurors here on Enki. Tanner shared how Qig had said that threat would be waived by one simple task—to somehow get the Words Muse leader, Uigoeri Qor, to lose the election for the new head juror position. While it had not been used, the murder of the Words Muse leader had been a consideration. Some of the team at the table squirmed in their seats at that comment. The diplomatic aides and the navy men knew about murder, as it was a part of their daily life in space, squirmed the most. "But we chose to not countenance murder," Tanner added, "so we— Bram and Kondo and I, tried to find another way to help Qig win the election."

Tanner continued with the planning process he, Bram, and Kondo had gone through and the solution they arrived at. The only way to avoid murder had been to somehow put Qor, the Words

Muse leader, in such a light that his reputation would be damaged. And what better way to do that, they found, than to use Bram's Issian skills to rig the chemical treatment of the food pellets that were supposed to turn a youngling's feathers to their muse colors. That had been even easier than they'd imagined, as Bram had found after testing that an Enkian could be controlled quite easily if one was close enough to them.

Some representatives made a data entry on their tablets, and the Faraway representative made notes on a pad of paper. *Wish I could have kept that one quiet, but no way now,* he thought.

Tanner sighed and continued with the last piece of the plan. "When the food was to be processed, just last week, Bram made his way to the Resources pyramid, gained entry, and used his skills as an Adept Officer to force the tech to think that he'd properly processed the food items. He did not, but he thought that he did, and the carts were then handled as always by the Resources section, delivered to the Words Muse pyramid, and administered at the big graduation night event last week."

Tanner took a sip of his tea, wishing for the days when a shot of his favorite Scotch would help. "And the next day, as we all knew," Tanner added, "the crap hit the fan, and at the big meeting in the

Words Muse rotunda the next day, the jurors informed us all about the investigation that they would be starting."

Everyone sat still, not a word was said. Some were still punching information into their tablets.

Tanner finished off by recapping the election just last night. "Our subterfuge must have worked as the Fine Arts Muse leader, Qig, was elected to the head juror position over the Words Muse leader, Qor. Everyone was happy," he said, "and that included us—until right after the election results were made public and fifty Militia soldiers invaded the *Atlas* with a warrant for Bram's arrest."

Tanner raised his hand to stop the questions and added that it was Bram who had stepped forward to accept the warrant and submit to the arrest, which had prevented Tanner from ordering that the Militia forces would be engaged by his *Atlas* marines. "That would have been a firefight in very close quarters, and while I had no doubt as to who would have won, there would have been casualties on our side."

Again, everyone tried to speak at once, and the ambassador knocked on the table to get everyone's attention. The ambassador waited for quiet before speaking.

"What we need to do here is to try to come up with a plan—a way to help Captain Scott to defend his lieutenant. And before you ask, you should all know that we have already supplied the captain, as the official from the defense side, to act as the counsel for Sander. So, ideas, please?" he said and then once again poised his finger above his tablet, ready to enter items.

There was quiet for a moment, and then the captain of the *Triumph*, the Duchy ship, started off.

"Do we get any kind of upfront proffer of evidence?" he asked.

Good question, Tanner thought.

Ambassador Harmon replied, "Asked and answered. They do not. The whole trial takes place in real time in front of the full five jurors. It will be prosecuted by the Words Muse leaders, we assume. But no, we get no upfront offer of the evidence that they have," he said.

None of the RIM representatives said a word.

"What is the burden of proof," one of the ambassador's aides asked.

"The prosecution must produce the evidence that will shift the conclusion of guilt away from the default position of innocence. Same as everywhere else, I'd imagine," the ambassador said.

That too was digested, and then Tanner spoke. "As I see it, here's what happens tomorrow. We go to the Words Muse pyramid for Bram's trial. At same, all evidence is presented as the prosecution sees fit. We get, we've been told, the ability to question witnesses, present our own too if we have any. No character witnesses allowed though, we are told. Simple, factual, and should be over in an hour, we were told. Fat chance," he said, his voice almost strident.

That got a few nods from around the table.

"Further, it is not 'til the trial actually starts that we even find out what Bram has been charged with, indictment-wise. Nor for that matter have they said any more than that, as that is Enkian justice, it appears," the ambassador said.

The ambassador ended the conference, and after a few nods and some keystrokes and tablet entries later, they all left.

Tanner sat with Kondo for a few minutes more.

"So, worst case, Sir?" Kondo said, "and how far will we go to ensure that Bram is found innocent? Or, do we also have a contingency plan in case the jurors find against us?" As he said that, he placed his tablet in front of Tanner.

On it, Tanner saw a simple list of all the *Atlas* combat troops on this mission to Enki. Listed were marines, Provost guards, EliteGuards, Air Force pilots, and more. The number was large, more than a thousand, but against a full planet of Militia soldiers, it wasn't enough. Tanner was about to mention that when Kondo slid the screen down a bit, and Tanner now noted that when one added in the Caliphate, UrPoPo, Duchy, and Faraway combat ready troops, the numbers hit almost ten thousand.

"That would be enough," Kondo said, "as we'd also take down AI robo-weapons too. I would think that at verdict time, if it went against us, we could fight our way out into the shuttles and up to the *Atlas* et al. with only minor casualties."

He sat back then, and they both stared at the tablet screen for quite a few minutes.

Tanner shook his head. "That, I'm afraid, we cannot do. Much as I'd like to just use our own forces to ensure that Bram goes free, we can't do that—yet. Note I said yet, Kondo, and I meant it. Instead, we will do our damnedest to defend our Adept Officer, and that should be enough," he said.

"Let's hope so," Kondo said as he swept the screen to blank, and they sat there lost in thought for the moment.

CHAPTER NINE

In the huge rotunda of the Words Muse pyramid, there was an issue with the seating. With every seat in the bleachers, the extra rollouts, and the huge floor taken, it was as if there wasn't an Enkian anywhere else but here. *Here for the trial of the century,* Tanner thought, as he and Kondo strode in the grade-level doors and stopped cold. Enkians. Several thousand, maybe even ten thousand, sets of eyes turned to stare at them. While he couldn't feel a thing other than anxiety, he knew disgust when he saw it. And it looked like the RIM, and more specifically, he and Kondo, had earned those stares of disgust.

He smiled broadly and clapped an arm around his XO's shoulder, and they walked together through the single aisle that was even narrower than usual due to the huge numbers of extra seats. All filled. All filled with Enkians of all muses, judging by the various feathered crest, each still staring at the two humans from the RIM. There were seats, he noted, for RIM parties too. There were some RIM members there from the *Pollux*, the Caliphate ship. The captain and a few others from the UrPoPo ship, the *Andiya*, more RIM members from the *Triumph* from the Duchy, and still more. They were seated on the floor, close to one side of the stage behind the table that would seat the defense team.

Finally reaching the stage, Tanner and Kondo climbed the short stairs, moved to the only empty side of the three tables set up in a triangular layout, and took two of the empty seats there. At the table to their left sat three Enkians—Words Muse citizens if one could count on the usual fact that a red and white feathered crest signified. One was the leader of the muse, Uigoeri Qor, the Enkian who had been the favorite in the election but who had lost to the Fine Arts Muse leader. Qor had lost the election on the strength of the loss of reputation after the feathered crest coloration failure. He nodded to Qor, the leader of the Words Muse, and the three of them stared at Tanner and Kondo. Again, the word disgust came to mind. They were going to be the prosecutors of the trial today, so

Tanner just smiled back and imagined them on the *Atlas* down on Deck Ten with wash buckets and mops. That made his smile even bigger, and he nodded to the Enkian in the middle.

He looked up at the huge view-screens that once again had been lowered from the ceiling, and he loved how big—really big—his smile looked on the screen. *Everyone will be able to see us with minute details—good to remember,* he thought.

"Game on," he said to himself as he looked at the other table. The other table was empty and awaiting the jurors. *But more importantly, where is my lieutenant?*

From the far side of the rotunda, near where the stairs were that went down to the access tunnels, a line of Militia soldiers appeared, marching in single file toward the stage. A conda led the men to completely circle the stage. As they took up picket duty, Tanner revisited his decision to come here today with Kondo only. No marines. No EliteGuards. No Provost guards. Just the defense team who had to win. That's all.

As the Militia was set a moment later, again from behind the same far wall, a small procession of the five jurors came out in single file, and they moved across the space, down the aisle, and then up onto the stage to take their seats at the empty table.

"Other than Bram, the stage is set," Tanner

whispered to Kondo, and they both sat and waited for whatever was to come next.

The newly elected head juror, Eecesoe Qig, rose, and his feathered crest, still proudly blue and red as he'd come from the Fine Arts Muse, fluttered broadly. That, as usual, quieted the whole rotunda, and he tapped the microphone to get their complete attention. *Like he didn't already have it*, Tanner thought.

"We, the jurors, declare this trial open. Please bring in the accused," he said loudly.

From across the rotunda, a Militia soldier came toward them, leading a small group behind him in single file. As they came closer, Bram could now be seen, as he too walked in the group. Upon reaching the stage, only the lead guard came up the stairs and then escorted Bram around to take his seat, the only empty one between Tanner and Kondo. The Militia officer then stepped back to remain on the stage but directly behind Bram.

"Bram, good to see you—you all right?" Tanner said as he shook the lieutenant's hand.

Bram nodded and said, "Fine, just a bit hungry is all. They don't have human food, and those dang pellets are awful." He grinned.

Tanner inspected him—not a mark he could see— his uniform was a bit wrinkled but still fine. No abuse from what he could see, but maybe the food

270

thing was a cruelty that he'd not yet considered. That almost made him smile, but he realized this was not the time for levity; he'd share that with Bram later after they'd won.

From the microphone, the head juror thanked the Militia for their attention to detail and then sat down at his seat.

The leader of the prosecution, Qor, rose to address the jurors. "We come before you today, jurors, to prosecute the defendant here," he said as he pointed at Bram, "with the charge of terrorism."

The rotunda exploded with caws, beak clicking, and calls of "string him up" and "guilty, guilty, the human is guilty ..." *All were signs,* Tanner thought, *that were not good for the defense.*

"Terrorism—Clerk, please enter the charges and note the trial has now begun," Qig said.

At the side of the stage but off and on the floor at a small table Tanner had not yet noticed, one of the seated Enkians responded, "Noted and continue, please."

Up on the stage, Qor held up his hand, and the talking in the rotunda slowly stopped. "As an opening statement, we—the Words Muse—on behalf of all of Enki, would like to say the following. That this charge of terrorism is the proper charge for what we know has happened here in the capital city. This human—Lieutenant

Bram Sander—has used his powers to somehow cancel our chemical treatment of the food pellets we use to indoctrinate our younglings. The first-ever massive dose of the coloration chemicals that changes the virgin white feathers of a youngling to their chosen muse colors. This was done with no regard to our Enkian customs and society. This was done, we know, to prevent our younglings from fully joining their chosen muse and becoming full citizens overnight. And this was accomplished by a human, who used his special skills, we will show, to further their human cause, the RIM Confederacy cause. We have witnesses that will tell all. There can be no doubt that this defendant is guilty and that we will ask for that guilty verdict," he finished off and sat at his place.

Qig, the head juror, nodded and then turned to Tanner. "Normally, this is where the defense—either the counsel or the defendant themselves—offers up an opening statement. Or, I might add as you do not really know our Enkian case procedures, this is where you can simply plead guilty too," he said as he looked right at Bram.

"Not guilty would be my plea," Bram said forcefully, and he slapped the table in front of him.

Everyone in the rotunda flinched as he did that, but one thing was for sure, everyone knew he meant it.

#####

Tanner moved the microphone closer to his face, and he thought for a moment before he began.

"It is my job, I understand, to help defend the lieutenant here, from charges that have been brought against him—that are false. And that is what I will do. So let's get started, shall we?" he said and then leaned back.

Out in the crowds in the rotunda, there were some very faint beak clicks and some shout-outs but too few to really make out what was being yelled.

Rising, Qor, the prosecutor, called his first witness. "Would Ambassador Harmon please come to the stage to give testimony," he said.

Tanner was on his feet immediately. "Wait," he said, "wait a minute here—that is a human RIM person—it's our ambassador. This should not be allowed," he stated forcefully to the jurors at the table facing him.

The head juror, Qig, nodded to him to indicate he'd heard Tanner, but then he held out a hand, palm facing him.

"You are not allowed, at least here on Enki, to protest about who is called as a witness. You too may call anyone you like," he said, and the beak clicking in the huge room was loud.

Ambassador Harmon slowly rose from his seat in

273

the audience and took the stage. He stopped though at their table and patted Bram on the arm as he stared at him, and then he moved to sit in the one seat off to one side of the tables and looked at the prosecutor with what Tanner thought was cautious concern.

"Ambassador Harmon, you have been in the RIM Confederacy Diplomatic Corps for how long?" Qor asked.

"For over forty years now, starting as a fresh graduate of the Juno University and rising now to be in the top echelon of the corps. My most recent posting was here, to Enki, to negotiate their entry in the RIM Confederacy," he said quietly.

"Yes, you are surely qualified, Ambassador. But my next question is not about you or the RIM; instead, I would like you to tell us all about the Issians, who come from Eons on the RIM. Would you give us your take on them—and their special skills?" Qor asked.

Ambassador Harmon was surprised, and yet as most diplomats, he would surely rise to the occasion.

"Yes, I can tell you about Eons and the Issians for days. But the short of it is the Issians are a small group of citizens from their planet Eons. They are very 'specialized' human beings. We still have no idea what gave them those special powers, but the following is true. They can read someone else's mind—"

A huge gasp and more beak clicking came from the rotunda crowd. He paused to let that lessen and after a few seconds, he continued.

"They have some better luck with some aliens and then not so much with others. They can also not only read a mind that they can link to, but they can also put in false memories into some brains too. They also, though we are told this is a very 'iffy' science, can see what lies in someone's future too. Sometimes just mere minutes, sometimes I've heard for days. As you may imagine, they are often wrong, so that puts this whole mindreading ability as a suspect set of skills. While I've no idea why, they also act as an Adept Officer in many navies on the RIM—the RIM Navy itself, the Barony Navy, the Conclusion Navy—there is quite a long list. Bottom line is—we just don't know if the skills are true or not. Sometimes yes and sometimes no," he finished off and smiled at the prosecutor, who nodded back as he was finished.

Tanner looked at the head juror and got a nod back, and he rose to question his ambassador.

"Ambassador Harmon, do you have any personal information that an Issian can in fact read minds? Anything that you know as you were involved in this somehow?"

Ambassador Harmon shook his head slightly. "Not at all, ever. What I related to you was simply what is bandied around on the RIM about the Issians. No one knows, for sure," he said and he was dismissed from the witness chair.

As Tanner sat, Bram leaned over and whispered in his ear, "Sir, the ambassador had one single word in his mind when he patted my arm—and he wanted me to see it. He said simply 'lose,' Sir."

As Tanner leaned back in his chair, that made him wonder why Harmon wanted them to lose. *He must know something that we don't. If only I could talk with him.* Knowing he couldn't talk to him right now, Tanner shook his head. *Why would he want us to lose this case?*

The prosecutor then called Resources Officer Swanki, the Enkian who had been in charge of the food processing treatment plant that handled the chemical immersion procedures.

More than five minutes of backstory about the process, how it was accomplished, and why it was necessary to so treat the food pellets that would initially colorize a set of white feathers into full muse colors in one evening too were covered. Qor asked many questions on the procedures as to what happened in the processing treatment room and how and why. He also drilled down a lot, Tanner thought, on the actual immersion process and how it was not run by any kind of Enkian AI. It was a manual chore, to simply hit a button, wait until the buzzer went off on the operator's console and then hit the button again. Qor also asked the tech how many times he'd done this before and received the answer of never.

"So this was your first time ever doing the immersion treatment then?" Qor asked.

Swanki confirmed he had never done this before, but he knew via his training and instructions from the treatment plant supervisor what to do and how to simply press a button.

Smiling, Qor then got to the meat of the testimony. "And on this day, when the immersion treatment occurred, were you alone in the treatment plant?"

"No, I was not, I had a visitor who said he had come down to see the immersion treatment, in person," Swanki said.

"And what did that person say to you—exact words, please, if you remember?"

"Yes, I remember what he said exactly as it was so nice. He said that he'd come to enjoy my first-ever food pellet immersion process and to congratulate me too. And I remembered how good that made me feel, so I thanked him and then pressed the button. A few minutes later, the tanks came back up, dripped out the excess chems, and they were done. I remember it well, Prosecutor," he said with pride even now.

"And, Officer Swanki, who was this person, this human, who came all the way over to the Resources pyramid, down into its depths, and into the food treatment process plant to stand beside you? Who was that person?" Qor said.

Swanki turned to look directly at Bram and pointed to him as he said, "Well, it was the defendant, Lieutenant Sander, who did that," and he smiled at his friend.

Again, there were gasps from the rotunda and much muttering drowned out the beak clicking that were louder than normal.

"Exactly, Officer Swanki, it was Lieutenant Sander, the Issian Adept Officer, who did that, wasn't it?" he said as he smiled at Bram. The prosecutor then smiled at Officer Swanki and said, "One more question, please ..."

Resources Officer Swanki nodded.

"Why is what the human said of such great interest, Officer Swanki?" Qor said.

"Because there was no way that he could have known that this was my first time, Prosecutor. I never told anyone that, ever. So the only way he could have known is by reading my mind," he added.

Beaks clacked, shout-outs happened, and

mutterings changed into yells as the rotunda suddenly exploded with noise and opinions.

Qig, the head juror, let it go for a moment and then looked at Tanner as if to ask if he had any comment or objection. Tanner sat still, saying nothing and looking down at his pad as he doodled in a corner. There was nothing to say here if he was to follow the ambassador's advice.

He leaned over to whisper into Bram's ear. "Are you positive that the ambassador said lose? One simple term for us to follow—lose?" he asked, his voice quiet but pointed.

Bram just nodded.

Tanner ignored the unspoken question on the head juror's face. Officer Swanki was relieved and the witness chair sat empty.

Tanner waited as the prosecutor seemed to be looking at the binder of notes in front of him, and Tanner was as surprised as anyone else when Qor said to the jury, "The prosecution rests, Your Honor," and then he sat down.

The head juror conferred with some of the other jurors and then turned back to his microphone. "Captain Scott, please present your defense of these charges," he said and sat back.

Everyone sat back to see what the defense counsel would do and what they'd be presenting as proof that the defendant was not guilty of terrorism.

Tanner pulled the microphone a bit closer and looked directly at the head juror. *Something else is afoot, I'm sure of that, but what?* He shook his head. *No time for that—the trial needed losing.*

"Your Honor and all the jurors. We have, as you also have, sat and listened to the evidence that was presented to yourselves as truth that there was enough evidence for the defendant to be guilty of terrorism. While the suitability of this charge is a topic for another day, what we heard—what we all heard—is conjecture, opinion, and conclusions based on gossip from the RIM, from a technician, and yes, from the prosecutor himself. We therefore ask that the jury would agree with us and issue an immediate and summary not guilty verdict." He leaned back in his chair and waited.

The head juror didn't even bother to confer with his other jurors. He said, "There will be no summary judgment in this case. Please present your defense, Captain," and he smiled.

Tanner shook his head and said into his microphone, "Then the defense rests, Your Honor. We do not believe that the prosecution has met their burden of proof, so we rest."

In the rotunda, the beak clacking and the mutterings started again. It was even happening at the prosecution table, and while Tanner wondered what it might be that they were discussing, he knew he'd never know.

The head juror nodded, spoke to one of his jurors for only a few seconds, and then looked back at the prosecutor. "Prosecutor, if you have a closing statement, please present it now," and he again leaned back.

Qor rose, looked at his notes, and then turned to face Bram. "You have done a major disservice to the Enkian people, Lieutenant Sander. You have, using your un-natural skills as an Issian, made a mockery of our most basic Enkian tradition—the graduation of our younglings into full muse adulthood. You did that. There is no question that you went down to the food treatment plant to ensure that the chemical immersions would not be completed. And out of your own mouth, you uttered the one thing you couldn't have known about Resources Officer Swanki, to prove your own mindreading meddling. You did this, Lieutenant, and I call upon our Enkian jurors to see that you are guilty and to ask for the most severe penalty of all, death. We ask for this lieutenant to pay the price of his guilt with his life—and we ask on behalf of all of Enki, jurors," he said, and he pushed the microphone away.

The crowd in the rotunda roared. Beaks were clacking like mad, there were deafening screams and yells, and chants of "Death, death, death," were also being made.

Tanner was in shock. At no time did he ever envision the penalty for this would be capital punishment. He looked at Bram who whispered one single word, "lose," and then he looked away.

Tanner nodded. Something else had to be afoot because if they lost, then Bram would die.

The head juror looked at him and said, "Does the defense have a final closing as well?"

Tanner nodded to Qig and then smiled. "As the head of the defense team for Lieutenant Sander, it falls to me to offer up only the following. As I have already stated, the prosecution has failed to make its case. This should be a simple task for the esteemed jurors to see as we all do—and find the lieutenant is innocent."

He sat and was quiet.

And he waited. They all waited, as the jurors rose and left the stage for their discussions.

#####

He turned to Bram and said, "We really didn't have a case, did we?"

His lieutenant shook his head.

"And if we'd have had a tape of the Fine Arts Muse trying to muscle us about the election, we'd have used it, wouldn't we?"

Bram nodded again.

"And yet, the ambassador must have his reasons

for asking us to stand down—not, to be honest, that we really had any cards to play."

Bram smiled. "I have no more information than you do," Bram said, "and with the thought of a death penalty being a part of all of this, all I can think of is that is exactly what the Ambassador said and that means—"

He stopped as a hand squeezed his shoulder, and he and Tanner turned around to see Ambassador Harmon standing behind them. He smiled at them and then squatted down to talk as surreptitiously as possible in the crowded rotunda. He leaned forward too so that his face could not be seen, and he said, "This is for us only—agreed?" as Kondo rose to stand directly behind him as a blocker of a sort.

Tanner said, "Lose? You wanted us to lose with a death penalty on the table?" He couldn't keep a tone of incredulousness from his voice.

Up above, the view-screens showed them conversing, but there was no audio. *Thank God.*

Harmon nodded. "I've been in talks with Qig, the head juror, since almost midnight. We struck a deal about a half hour before the trial started, and here's what you need to know. Sander will be found guilty, but Qig will not allow the death penalty to be applied. Instead, it is a lifetime banishment from Enki. We will simply take him up to the *Atlas*, and he's never to return. That left Qig some face-saving room as it was him that got this all started with the threat to us to help him rig the election, which we did. He wants that buried and so do we. Qor is none the wiser by the way," he said under his breath, "and we want that to remain the same too."

Tanner nodded but something stood out in all of this. "Ambassador, one thing? The probe metal, the Xithricite? What about that?"

The Ambassador nodded and smiled. "Hence the long, long discussions. We reached agreement on the lieutenant in an hour—but it took more than seven more to gain at least some standing with that one. We will be able to get twenty-five percent of their ore output, on an annual basis. And yes, we had to let them know that the metal has some great value to those of us who have advanced technology —we did not reveal its true value, of course. And yes, we all know that this is a small amount, so the Enkians have nicely agreed to allow us to provide better technology in the mining of those ores only— to begin with. That, we estimate, will increase the ore tonnage by about four hundred percent. They, however, get the technology for free, of course, as the first of the many ways that the RIM can help Enki move into this millennium."

They all nodded.

"And FTL?" Bram added.

"Ahh ... yes, the crux of new technology, FTL ... but that's not even on the table yet. Here they come," he added as he slowly stood up as the jurors were coming back to the stage.

"Out for less than a half hour—would a real lawyer be worried about that?" Tanner mused.

"No way to know," Bram said as the ambassador left the stage area to return to his seat and the jurors climbed the stairs to take their seats.

The head juror rose now, and his feathered crest rippled and rippled. The crowds eventually noticed and sat, and silence broke out in the rotunda.

Qig stared at them all on the stage, first at the prosecution and then at the defense team, and finally at Bram himself. "Would the accused please rise," he said.

Bram, Tanner, and Kondo all stood and faced the table of jurors.

"After much reflection and the weighing of the evidence, we, the jurors, find the defendant, Lieutenant Sander, guilty as charged with terrorism."

The rotunda went crazy with loud shouts and beaks clacking, and again, the chant of "Death, death, death," could be heard.

Qig, waited until the crowd quieted and then went on. "We therefore herewith impose the penalty of death to the guilty defendant to be

285

carried out within the week," he said, and the crowd roared with delight.

Tanner thought that he'd misheard Qig and looked to Bram who was frozen in his chair.

"Militia, please take the guilty party back into custody." Qig sat once more in the head juror's chair.

Tanner half-rose but couldn't be heard over the tumult that was going on in the rotunda. Enkians from the audience were climbing up the stairs to congratulate the prosecutor or the jurors perhaps, he didn't know, but suddenly he wished he had worn his sidearm, as some turned toward the defense table. *Thank God.* The Militia soldiers on picket duty had stepped up and were pushing off the Enkians who had no business on the stage. A small squad put cuffs back on Bram and began to move him out of the rotunda and back to the Militia pyramid.

Before he left, Tanner leaned over. "Don't despair, Bram, I'm on this and on this with all the might of the RIM," he said, and as Bram nodded, Kondo nudged Tanner.

"Sir, the ambassador is waving at us—we should go too," he said, and they got in behind the soldiers as they left the stage.

Once down on the floor, they had to push a little and move chairs out of their way, but eventually they reached the ambassador who said, "Upstairs to the offices," and he turned to work his way out of the crowd to the far side of the rotunda.

CHAPTER TEN

Lieutenant Cooper, at the helm on the bridge, tried to signal the Air Force wing commander, as he strode onto the bridge, but he never caught the officer's eye.

Colonel David Richards marched straight up to the captain's chair to speak to his captain. "Sir," he said."Colonel, what are you doing on the bridge without asking for an admit to same?" Tanner said, his voice fierce and his glare aimed straight at the now uncomfortable colonel.

"I ... I didn't know that I had to—" he said but was interrupted by the captain.

"XO, what regulation in the Barony Navy regs did our colonel here just breach?" he barked out.

Kondo had his fingers flying on the keyboard, and if one looked, they would have seen a long scrolling page of fine print rolling across his console monitor.

"Sir, yes ... sorry, Sir, for the delay—that would be Navy Regulations on Bridge Deportment, um, Article Eleven, but I don't yet see—"

"Never mind, XO," Tanner barked once more, and he looked instead at the Air Force colonel. "What is it, Colonel, my lunch is about due from the stewards," he said as his wing commander visibly came to attention, and his face looked like it was carved out of stone.

"Sir, yes, Sir. I just wanted—sorry, Sir. I am here to report that our first Air Force military exercise have been ongoing and quite successful, we believe, as well, Sir. Just got the debriefings, Sir." He handed a set of printed reports to Tanner. "We had more than one hundred and fifty of our single, double, and even troop carriers down on Enki as per our plans. While there was no actual combat, we showed what kind of a combatant we would be to all onlookers, and, Sir, I've sent through some fighter display footage if you'd care to see it?"

Tanner nodded to his helm officer, and moments later on the huge bridge view-screen, suddenly they were flying over Enki, the brown sands far below.

His fingers were tapping one, two ... one, two on his knee. He was under stress now, as Bram's future—Bram's life—was at stake. He turned back to the screen.

As this fighter flew along in the distance, a set of pyramids slowly grew along the horizon, and the fighter seemed to slow, as passing it now were dozens of other fighters, both singles and doubles too. They moved off at a terrific rate, and the camera fighter climbed to get above the conflagration below near what could be seen was the capital city of Enki.

While the exercise included no adversary squadrons, it was understood that this was not a combat dogfight exercise but instead a bombing exercise. Wave after wave of the fighters took a low bombing run at the central pyramid of the city, the Resources pyramid. At no time, one could see, was there any real threat to the pyramid itself, as the singles took straight runs at it. The doubles, instead of using a straight run, took spirals down toward the central pyramid, pulling up and out of the way at the last instant.

"Impressive," Tanner said. "How close did those doubles get?" he asked.

"Sir," Colonel Richards said, "I got within twenty feet of the pyramid myself, and a few got a bit closer. There was no doubt that we showed anyone watching what kind of a foe we would be, Sir. And here's a look at those who came out into the sunshine to watch, Sir."

The camera fighter then took a long, low, slow pass between two of the outlying pyramids, aimed at the center one, the Resources pyramid, the surrogate target for the exercise. As it passed over the gap between the two outer pyramids, one could see down on the sand hundreds, maybe thousands, of small figures of Enkians staring up at the whole wing of fighters. Faces looked up, feathered crests were blown by the fighters, and all those faces showed one thing.

Fear.

Fear of something they'd never seen before.

Fear of what such a force could do should that need to happen.

"Time of the exercise?" Tanner intoned.

"At 0930 hours, Sir. Lasted a full hour, Sir. Complete tape is in the wing archives too, Lieutenant," Richards said to the helmsman

Tanner shook his head. *No need to see the tape yet.*

"And tomorrow's exercise, Colonel?" he barked out.

"Sir, same hour but this time, we're using our bomber forces—more than two hundred of them, and the exercise again will use the Resources pyramid as the surrogate target. We are going to speed up the rate of fire—well, pseudo-fire, actually —to enable us to make more than four runs as well as to also use troop transports to land a full division of marines, Sir. If it's one thing we Barony military men know, it's how to fight, Sir. And that's exactly what we will show Enki tomorrow once more. Oh, and, Sir, plans are underway for a combined land/air and bomber exercise now, Sir. We'll forward same to you within the hour, Sir," he said, still standing at attention and staring straight ahead.

Tanner nodded. "Dismissed, Colonel," he said and told the helm to kill the streaming.

After a second or two, the screen went back to show the planet below, slowly turning in orbit beneath them. He pondered the recently finished exercise and wondered what it might have meant to the Enkians below. It had been only a bit less than twenty-four hours after the guilty verdict at Bram's trial yesterday. He knew that tomorrow's exercise would be bigger, flashier, and hopefully more on-point.

He was on edge, he knew, as his fingers slowed and tapped one, two ... one, two ... on his knee.

Lieutenant Irving, the bridge Ansible officer, turned and said, "Sir, incoming EYES ONLY from the ambassador down in the capital city. Ready room, Sir?" she asked.

"Roger that, STAT," he said as he jumped up and ran across the bridge to his ready room just off to one side of the bridge.

He sat at his desk, and the monitor on his console

suddenly lit up, and the face of the ambassador appeared.

"Captain, good news. I have just been asked to come to meet with the jurors on a 'matter of great importance,' I was told. In twenty minutes. I have also been told that I am the only one whom they will meet with—so I called you immediately to let you know. I will gain Bram's freedom over all else —is that our wish, Captain?"

Tanner nodded. He would have liked to be there. But yes, that was the main thrust of the meeting. Bram's freedom.

Ambassador Harmon smiled—not a big broad smile, but a small one. "I will gain that goal—and you should also know that there are Enkians in all the muse pyramids screaming at their leaders for protection against the RIM aggressors. Your exercise seemed to help—while I would have argued against, it had I known, it did cause some fears down here. I will add that to my bag of diplomatic tricks, Captain. Kudos," he said.

Tanner smiled broadly and he wondered what the Enkians would think about tomorrow's planned exercise and the combined assault exercise the day after.

"I will be back to you STAT, Captain—wish me luck," the ambassador said.

"Sir, the Enkians need more than luck if they

293

wish to have a planet should you not be successful. No doubt about that, Sir," he said and his voice was loaded with emotion as his fingers beat out the one, two ... one, two rhythm on his knee.

#####

In his quarters, Tanner sat at the desk and wished he could still get drunk. That would have made this time all the easier to handle, but alas, that single shot months back on the Barony Hospital Ship had cured his alcoholism.

Still, anything was better than sitting and staring at Enki as it slowly rolled along in its orbit below the *Atlas*, the browns of the sands, the bands of green in its northern latitudes, and the white clouds much more prevalent up there.

He played with a hangnail, gnawing at it with his teeth, worrying it away from his finger.

The ambassador had been at the meeting for over an hour. And as yet, no word.

Oh, for a Scotch, he thought. *Or maybe something else? Alcohol was out. But there were drugs. Most simply made you high at first. Then the real price had to be paid.* And that didn't appeal to him at all.

How about love? They said that being in love was a high that was without parallel. He wondered if that was true. For a moment, he thought of Tibah, and he was sorry about how things had ended up; yet he had done what had to be done. The Lady came to mind then; he liked her, very much indeed. She was a Royal, and that was a whole different issue. Still, he thought that she liked him too, old as he was. That gave him a thought, as to what he was going to do to help celebrate his upcoming fortieth birthday. *Maybe she could join him for a dinner or the like. Maybe ...*

He snorted. Here he was, making plans for a birthday with a Royal and his best friend was—
BEEP!

The console monitor beeped at him again, and he quickly told the AI to answer it.

The ambassador's face came on screen, with no smile at all. He held out his hands, palms up—and then he smiled. "We had to give up the truth about the probe metal—what's their name for it—Xithricite. We had to also tell them the full story on that, which I did against my better judgment, but Qig is no idiot. He knew if we were pushing for an ore, that there was something up with that," he said and the smile was still there.

Tanner nodded.

"They have commuted the lieutenant's sentence from death to banishment for life. He is to never ever come back to Enki. Further—we also have gained a full fifty percent of the Xithricite," he said and smiled more broadly.

Tanner nodded and asked, "And the lieutenant?"

"Militia is in the process of delivering him back to the *Atlas* in the next little while. I suggested that they do just that—hope that's okay?"

Tanner nodded and said, "Roger that, Ambassador."

The ambassador went on. "So, we have a deal. Enki is a new member of the RIM Confederacy— oh, forgot to mention that Qor, the Words Muse head, was also at that meeting, and he concurs with all of this. Of course, it was him that held up the deal for FTL so that his muse would get that frigate, but I expect that should have been foreseen. In any event, all the ducks here are in a row—no pun intended, Captain."

"So," Tanner said, "are we good to go? Once Bram is back onboard, I'd very much like to get back to the Barony, and that would be okay, right?" "We'd send down your own things from your quarters here on the *Atlas*, though, Ambassador," he offered.

"Not needed—I took them with me down here to Enki just yesterday, figuring that you would want to hightail it out of here soonest. And yes, Captain, you are good to go. My thanks for all of your help, and a soft point? What happens on a diplomatic mission is different for each of same. This was no harder nor no easier than any other. You have my own personal thanks on your help and counsel too. Good man, Captain Scott," he said, and he half-saluted Tanner as he said that.

Tanner nodded and clicked off the connection.

Bram was safe and on the way back.

He moved quickly now, leaving his quarters up on Deck Four, and loping along the deck corridor, he quickly went down the stairs two at a time and then turned forward to get to the bridge. As he entered, Lieutenant Commander Sheldon, the Science officer on the bridge, called out, "Captain on the bridge."

Tanner waved off the salutes and took his seat. "Helm, plot me a course to the Barony, quickest and shortest, lad—and let me know when the candle is lit," he said. "XO, please have a squad of marines down in the landing bay—Lieutenant Sander is released and being delivered back to us in minutes."

A huge hurrah came from every officer on the bridge. Tanner smiled and nodded to them as the crew hooted for a few more seconds.

"Yes, good work by the RIM ambassador got him freed. Well, banished is the proper term ... never to be able to return to Enki—talk about a bonus too!" He smiled, as there were more hoots too, and nodded along as the XO started up a "Three cheers for the ambassador," and the bridge celebrated for a bit.

Time to get a move on, he thought, *back to the RIM*
...

#####

Tanner kicked off the sheet and then lay on his
side, feeling the cooling effect of evaporation as the
sweat on his back slowly whispered away. He'd
slept about an hour or so, and now he'd lain awake
for more than two hours more, his mind working
and working and keeping sleep at bay.

He lifted up his head and punched his pillow,
trying to get it puffier in the middle, and he flopped
his head back down on the not-right pillow. He
kicked one leg out from under the tail end of the
sheet to try to cool off, and within two minutes, he
was cold and had to pull the sheet back over him.
He shivered for a moment until he warmed up.

What am I going to do with my life? he thought in
an existential moment.

Wait, no ... If he remembered correctly from his
philosophy course from almost twenty years ago,
the existential part was not true. He wasn't looking
at the very foundations of his life: whether this life
had any meaning, purpose, or value, which was
what the existential part referred to.

Instead, what was bugging the hell out of him
was his lack of real purpose—at least something he

could hang his hat on as a goal in life.

He didn't want to turn forty in a few weeks. He didn't want to sit out on life.

He switched sides to lie facing the far wall and ignored the big photo he'd had his steward put up of the *RN Marwick* floating above some planet he couldn't remember.

He wanted to fall in love and have a child or three. He wanted to find out if a captaincy was his ultimate navy rank.

He pulled his arm out from below the pillow and draped it across his hip.

He didn't want to feel like he was feeling right now.

Scotch, he thought, *would have made things so much easier. Put me in a glow where nothing really mattered that much.*

He rolled over on his back, pushing the sheet down to his waist, and threw an arm over his forehead.

Life is difficult—no more so out on the RIM, I know. But still something to be considered ... like I don't have enough to worry about and fear.

He sat upright when he thought about the word fear—and how the Lady had used it to describe those refugees on KappaD.

More scared about what lay behind them than ahead.

He rolled over, tucked his arm beneath his pillow once more, and tried for the hundredth time to go back to sleep.

Epilogue ~

Captain Abu al-Hasan leaned back on his captain's chair on the *CN Pollux*, smiled at the big face of his Caliph on the bridge view-screen in front of him, and nodded too. "Caliph, yes, we have gotten almost all that we were after—at a cost as you know that was in the range that you gave us to negotiate with as well," he said, and he ticked off the items one by one of his fingers.

The citizens of the Caliphate were a tall alien race who were always over six and half feet tall, so sitting down even, they still looked taller than most. The Caliphate, a full member of the RIM Confederacy, was a realm with nine planets. There had been ten, but Olbia had revolted, and the upcoming referendum on their freedom was coming up soon too.

The Caliph nodded and looked at his captain.

The captain continued. "Sire, as you indicated, we were able to have private talks with the heads of all of the cults—well, they call them muses here on Enki. And each of them found something to ask for, for our support and help. Each of them was a hard set of negotiations, but all succumbed to the lure of spreading their cult—muses—within the RIM," he said, and the Caliph nodded.

"Further, when we sat with the jurors—the group

that really is the head of the planetary government here on Enki—they too were willing to negotiate. Mostly, I think that we were used to vet what work the ambassador had completed with them. They asked us to qualify every single item that they had worked out to join the Confederacy. But, as you surmised, they were more than willing to become the newest member of the Caliphate instead, once we made them a bigger offer than the ambassador could make. We gave them FTL, Caliph, and you were right, it was the deciding factor."

He smiled at his Caliph, who just stared back at him solidly.

The captain sat, and while nothing more was said, he grew nervous.

He had followed the directions he had been given exactly. He had dealt with the Enkians in charge using his best ability and had for the most part been able to get what his Caliph had wanted—a new member of the Caliphate.

He sat and fiddled with his leg, crossed over the other. It bounced and he pulled it down to set his foot firmly on the bridge deck.

"Sir, have I done something wrong?" he asked quietly.

The Caliph stared at him for another minute before speaking. "Captain, you have done fine—as you were directed to, and I'm pleased to see that we will have a brand new member of the Caliphate realm, which is now back to our original total of ten planets," he said as he smiled.

"I think the Baroness has a surprise coming," he said to no one in particular as the connection with the *Pollux* was broken and the captain's screen faded to black.

BOOK SEVEN OF THE RIM CONFEDERACY

Ruined Memories

Prologue ~

It sat rock still, this large terraforming foundry with the dust of centuries on it's skin. It should be moving as a part of it's task, but instead it was unpowered. Wonder what she'd be like when she has power, the merchant marine third mate thought, as he yanked even harder on the cables. Attached to the big transformer that now sat alone on the skid dolly, the cables usually transferred the power to the unit, but not anymore. Or ever, the third mate thought—this terraformer had never even been turned on as far as anyone on his ship, the *Scavenger*, a merchant marine freighter, could tell. While this was their first trip to this terraformer, they'd already stripped one completely of everything salable in the past year and this was their number two foundry.

Pretty easy to tell, he said to himself as he jammed a foot against the edge of the cable port and worried the lines back and forth trying to get them to unhook. When you land a terraformer, it moves. And it leaves a very noticeable trail behind it as it did it's job of turning an uninhabitable planet into one that you could colonize. This one had only unmarked grass and weeds around it; it had never ever moved for as long as it had been here on the planet Memories.

Probably part of it he thought as he chewed on his lip, he strained and then yanked and yanked harder again, is that this dumb planet, with no sentient s on it, was tucked in a pocked in the huge nebula that lay south of the RIM Confederacy. Between the RIM and the Pentyaan empire, the nebula was thick, heavily loaded with particulate matter—in fact a danger for most to enter. Not us, nor for that matter whomever had delivered all of these terraformers either; we found this planet almost a year ago. And we still raid the planet to steal equipment and rare earths and salvage whatever we can, time and time again.

Pop-pop!

The sound of the cables letting go somewhere behind the bulkhead was the first thing he felt as he stumbled over backwards and fell on the floor of the storage room. As he slowly got back up, he noted that the cables in his hand now ended with some kind of plugs that he'd been able to pull out of the connection hidden behind the bulkhead. He smiled as he coiled them up and then hung them on top of the transformer so that he'd be able to roll the dolly down the short corridor to his left and get it to where he could dump the whole thing out of the side port of the terraformer.

Once it hit the ground, some of the crew would drag it towards the *Scavenger* and then hoist it up and into the hold. This transformer he knew, had more than six thousand credits worth of rare earth magnetics in it that they'd strip out during the trip back to the RIM and sell on KappaD and space the junk.

Turning back towards the storage room, he looked inside and took a quick inventory of what was left. There were still three more of these transformers or whatever the hell they were called; three huge spools of some kind of fiber that he thought might have something to do with lasers maybe and more than dozens of some kind of bags of purple gel. No idea what it was for and they'd found out on KappaD on the last trip, no one wanted to buy them either. A huge round insulated column sat right in the middle of the floor that he knew was somehow connected to the laser and as he looked around it, he noticed something odd—a set of lights had suddenly lit up along one wall, in the ceiling. As he looked at that, the floor suddenly began to vibrate a little, then a little more.

He felt a lurch and that scared him.

A lurch meant—as any space man knew, that they were underway—but this was not a ship, it was a terraforming foundry.

Someone had started up this huge arena sized machine and as he pounded down that corridor once more towards the side door, he could now see the very slowly moving ground drifting by.

This thing is moving . . .he said as he knew it would soon be laser drilling down into the ground of Memories, with a laser that was more powerful than one might imagine. It had taken them almost six months to learn that they couldn't salvage that on their first foundry they'd picked apart. They had learned that the laser was used to drill down up to three miles as it searched for what was on it's AI list; ores of a certain type and radioactivity along with minerals that were needed for formation of atmospheric compounds that were also needed to get Memories ready for colonization.

They also had learned that all of the foundries had lain dormant for more than thousands of years until just a few moments ago at least for this one. He clicked on his PDA and the *Scavenger's* on duty deck cadet sounded scared but did confirm that yes, the terraformer was underway at about six feet per second. He had no idea on the others that they'd already recorded location wise though. The third mate made a choice. He had to get out of this foundry and that meant that he'd have to go down the rope ladder as it was slowly swaying the thirty feet to the ground. It was something any able bodied seaman would be expected to be able to do —he just hoped he could too. He spun and slowly lowered a leg down so that his foot reached the first rung, and as he found it, he then lowered his other leg and slowly began to move down the ladder. He had already made three more rungs down wards when the terraformer stuttered to a halt and that made him miss a rung and he swung freely by only his hands.

No more than five feet away from him, an orange laser beam from above suddenly appeared, with it's more than five petawatts of power, it was like the searing power of a sun almost close enough to touch.

It turned the third mate into a cinder in a millisecond as it drilled down deep into the planet below. It boiled everything it met and it read the chromatics of the ores that came back and then recording the location for later machines that were on their way to the planet.

Around the terraforming foundry, the air of course, was barely that; very high in carbon dioxide, it made the planet a hothouse but that didn't matter much as it was uninhabited. Not a single sentient species on the globe though it was full of what could be called normal predator prey animals. Thick air, now horribly smelling of burned vegetation, peat, ores of unknown type and soil, rock and the third mate too.

The laser snapped off; it's trillions of watts suddenly gone.

The foundry slowly started up it's movements again. Ahead of it lay a continent's worth of laser drilling and testing the ores it needed. They were quickly liquefied and the resulting up-welling of the gas billowed and behind it was now only one such vented hole.

This terraforming foundry had sat idle for thousands of years; now it would move along it's path doing it's job, making this planet a colonization candidate.

Available in the Winter of 2016!

Want to get early notice when we've got a new RIM Confederacy Series book launch?

Just drop by www.jimrudnick.ca and leave you email address and we'll let you know!

Or drop by our FaceBook page at www.facebook.com/theRIMConfederacy/

Would you like to leave me a Review?

Dear Reader…

If you've made it this far, you're most likely thinking that this was the best SciFi you've ever read.

Or maybe not.

Maybe Captain Scott wasn't your cup of tea?

Or you hate the Baroness and her scheming ways?

Or does the Caliph look like an upcoming tyrant?

So I'd like to ask you for a favor?

Would you mind taking a few minutes to write a review for me please?

And I'm talking honest too! Nothing makes us writers get better than book reviews!

Your comments help others know what to expect when they're looking for a great SciFi read...

If you want to write on any of the three books in this RIM Confederacy BoxSet then just click one of the links below...

And thanks once again, I'm looking forward to reading your comments!

Jim Rudnick
2016